Clara & Pig

MARY ANN TIPPETT

Text copyright 2018 by Mary Ann Tippett
All rights reserved

ISBN 978-1-7753883-0-2 (book)
ISBN 978-1-7753883-1-9 (ebook)

For those who grapple with the fleeting bits of mind that travel between memories like butterflies on flowers.

"*The Greek word for 'return' is nostos. Algos means 'suffering.' So nostalgia is the suffering caused by an unappeased yearning to return.*"

—*Milan Kundera,* **Ignorance**

"*People always talk about how hard it can be to remember things - where they left their keys, or the name of an acquaintance - but no one ever talks about how much effort we put into forgetting. I am exhausted from the effort to forget... There are things that have to be forgotten if you want to go on living.*"

—*Stephen Carpenter,* **Killer**

Chapter 1

The squirrel hangs like a horrific piece of art. "Modern" art, Clara thinks. The kind meant to stir up controversy. The creature is at least ten feet up, reddish brown, mouth wide open in an agonizing display of teeth. It is crucified, all four taloned limbs stretched out toward the world, its back mercilessly fixed to the tree.

Seconds before the squirrel sighting, she had started a cigarette, waiting for Pig to poop. Clara prefers the clandestine thrill of smoking inside. But Peter, her son, pointed out the smoking area across the lot from Milton Manor's garage. His implication was clear. He thinks she doesn't want to meet people. He's right, of course. She hates Vermont, does not plan on staying, and has zero desire to befriend anyone, let alone spend her twilight years in such a liberal and abysmally cold place. But now that he's pointed it out, she has to prove him wrong.

Pig had been snuffling about beneath a giant pine tree, having dragged her further from the garage than she intended. Clara had pulled out her smokes in part to avoid watching Pig poop, but mainly because the pine offered some relief from the wind that crept down her neck and through every button of her Kate Spade peacoat.

Now the cigarette dangles unsmoked from her fingers. Who

did this, she wonders, intending to look away. Her eyes stubbornly betray her intent. Pig tugs at the leash to head back, but Clara's feet stay glued to the ground.

A too chipper of a voice behind her sings out a greeting and something about a bag. Clara ignores her. "Hi there," she shrills too close to Clara's ear. "You got any poop bags?"

Clara fills her lungs with air and noisily breathes it out before turning. "What's a poop bag?" Chipper woman lacks fashion sense, Clara observes. Appalling pleather boots and a medley of grey layers and scarves assault her senses when she finally turns around.

Remembering her mission to prove Peter wrong, Clara promptly extends her leashed hand, introduces herself. "And this is Pig. He's a pug."

"I'm Bonnie," comes the voice from inside the scarves. "You just moved in, right? How are you settling in?"

Having accomplished her mission of meeting someone new, Clara ignores the questions and turns back to the squirrel. "Who do you think would do such a thing?" Her hand with mostly ash clinging to it, points up the tree.

"What, oh, wow, I..." is all Bonnie gets out, as they both gaze upwards, mesmerized.

Clara hears heavy footsteps and turns to see a man walking past. She recognizes him from the lobby. He had been holding court with a gaggle of seniors, mostly women, gossiping in plain view as she followed the movers through the code-activated double doors and up the elevator on what ranks highly as one of the worst days of her life. "You're the lobby guy!" Clara shouts at him. "Thanks for not opening the door for me last week!"

Lobby guy stops, chuckles, makes his way back up the

U-shaped driveway. "I don't remember you asking for help," he says.

"I didn't know gentlemen needed to be asked," Clara fires back.

"Touché," he says in one syllable rather than two, and extends his hand. "Name's Jimmy, by the way. And to whom do I have the pleasure of meeting this crisp November morning?"

"'Who' do you have the pleasure," corrects Clara. "This is Bonnie. I'm Clara. And if you're not too busy gossiping and failing to open doors, perhaps you could explain what kind of hooligans run around this depraved neighborhood?"

Jimmy's smile remains as he drops his hand to pet the pug straining to make his acquaintance. "Kind of a fat little fella, arntcha?" he says, giving Pig some ear rubs, prompting Pig to lean into him, offering up his bum for scratches. "I don't take your meaning," Jimmy says to Clara with a wink.

"'Whom' is right," Bonnie chimes in. Clara gives Bonnie an icy look. Bonnie points to the tortuous scene up the pine's trunk, and Jimmy aims his baseball cap skyward. "I'm sure this was some kind of accident, don't you think?"

The three of them stand there in silence, surveying the squirrel's predicament. Clara pulls her collar up, crosses her arms and sees her stub of a cigarette has gone out. She starts to toss it on the ground and remembers Bonnie's poop bag question. Such rudeness. They've only just met, and she's already nagging about poop and grammar. That's what I get for trying to meet people, Clara thinks with an audible huff.

"Well," Jimmy finally says. "It's dead. That's for sure."

"Murdered," Clara corrects.

"Strange it's brown, not grey," Bonnie says.

Jimmy and Clara look at Bonnie quizzically. Bonnie fails to elaborate. "Why would a squirrel be grey?" Clara finally asks.

Bonnie opens her mouth to laugh, as if they made a joke. Her eyes widen in surprise when she sees their serious expressions. "I guess you aren't Vermonters. Been in Vermont all my life. Never seen a brown one around here."

"Ever seen one stuck in a tree?" Clara asks.

"Never seen that either."

"Well," says Jimmy in a there-you-have-it kind of tone.

Clara notices Jimmy's short sleeves and blue jeans with holes. Crazy way to dress in this weather, she thinks. "Definitely murdered."

"Well," Jimmy says again. "I'm off to the diner. There's a stack of flapjacks with my name on it."

Clara's fingers have gone from tingly to numb, and frankly she is done with this conversation anyway. "I hate it here," she says to no one in particular and gives in to Pig's persistent tugs back toward the building.

"You forgot your poop," she hears Bonnie chirp after her. Clara throws her cigarette butt on the pavement and disappears into the garage.

Chapter 2

"When can I drive my car?" Clara asks Peter.

He finishes parceling out her pills amongst the compartments of a pill box the size of Texas. She is feeling cagy inside her beige three-roomed apartment. It doesn't help that one room is crammed to the gills with boxes. Her heart sinks when she ponders the treasures within those boxes that gleamed proudly in her Florida mansion. Vermont and this crummy rat hole of a place are not good enough for such treasures. It makes her sick to even think about unpacking them.

Peter eyes her sympathetically. His hair is thinner than she remembered, and she wonders when the edges started to grey. "It needs a tune-up at the very least," Peter says. "The movers thought it might be on its last legs. It isn't safe. And anyway, you need to get a Vermont license plate."

Clara just stares at him icily, surprised by the hint of tears burning in her nose, waits for an answer she can accept.

"Let's go through a box or two while I'm here, okay Mom? Then we can head out for breakfast. Sound good?"

"I hate it here," Clara replies. "People are mean. One of them called Pig fat. Can you believe that? He walked right up to me and said, 'Your dog is fat.'"

"Hmmm," is all Peter can say and heads toward the spare

room. The sound of scissors slicing open a box makes her nauseous.

Clara looks at the pill box. It has three rows breaking up the days of the week, for morning, noon and night. She glances up over the bar and to the cabinets above the kitchen where her clock should be. She has no idea what time it is. She is stuck in a bleak nothingness of time. A time between where she once was and where she intends to be again.

Anxiously, she begins pushing in chairs to the dining room table that juts out awkwardly from the living room wall. She picks up a few of Pig's toys and places them in the bin. Pig looks up from his nap on the couch a few feet opposite the table and watches her warily as she folds and refolds the blankets she keeps nearby.

The TV in the corner drones quietly, words spilling across the bottom of the screen. She wants a cigarette but won't smoke in front of Peter. He knows she smokes. But she can't stand the judgment. He seemed so impressed all those years ago when she told him over the phone she had quit. He lived so far away and rarely visited, so what did it matter?

"Do you want any of this stuff?" Peter asks from the other room. She peers around the corner and sees him pulling out some pottery she remembers buying with her friend Liz. When Max died, Liz filled the dreary gaps in Clara's week by dragging her out for lunch in little towns close by. She found relief in the local shops, laughing at the witty cocktail napkins and preserving the moments with decorative bobbles for her shelf or coffee table from each outing. Her mind drifts to Liz's walk with cancer and she refuses to yield to it.

"No," Clara says, "you take it. Give it to the homeless." Her heart lifts, imagining a person in need enjoying these treasures as she once did.

Peter takes out the treasures one by one and sets them in the tiny hallway in front of the bathroom. "How about we start a donate pile and a trash pile? I can bring the trash downstairs today. There must be a dumpster around here. I'll come back for the give-away pile next week."

The sparkle in the pieces he sets down is all wrong. The dreary beige around her steals the life from them. She looks away. Feels ashamed.

"I'm out of bread," she says, suddenly wanting Peter to leave.

He stomps on the empty box to flatten it and gathers up the filler newspaper balls, stuffing them into a garbage bag. "We can hit the grocery after breakfast," he says.

Something in her snaps. "I hate it here," she says. Her words hit him without impact like an echo. "I HATE it," she says louder. "People are mean. It's cold. Why couldn't you leave me in Florida to die? I have a car, you know. I can leave any time." With each phrase her voice gets louder, shakier, more shrill.

"Because," he says with no emotion, like he has said it a hundred times and doesn't care anymore how it affects her, "you have nowhere to live in Florida. You stopped paying your bills. You were taking pills randomly. You broke your wrist. Then separated your shoulder. Then cracked your head coming out of Walmart. I can't help you from so far away."

"I didn't ask for your help." She is powerless against the tears now streaming down her face, her chest heaving. "I hate it here. I know how you are. I know you. You have always been this way. So controlling like your father. I want to die. I don't want to be here."

Peter tries to hug her, but she backs up and grabs a tissue

from the coffee table. "Mom, if you keep saying you want to die, I will have to take you to Emergency. I won't be able to leave you alone. I know it's hard..."

The door bell rings and Pig barks, aroo-roo-roo, streaking to the door like a pudgy rocket. Clara steps into the bathroom to gather herself while Peter scoops up Pig to quiet him.

From the bathroom, Clara hears Bonnie's annoyingly cheerful voice oozing all over her son. She blows her nose and quickly pats the tears from her eyes. "Hello, Bonnie," she says as normally as possible, the three of them meeting in the kitchen just inside the apartment door. "This is my best friend, Bonnie," Clara says to Peter. He raises an eyebrow. See, I don't need help, she wants to say; in fact, I already have a best friend, that's how okay I am. Bonnie looks up at Peter, then at Clara, unsure of what to say. "We bonded over a dead squirrel," Clara says.

Bonnie looks better without all the grey layers, Clara notices. Her eyes are a soft brown, her hair salt and pepper (she imagines it was long and jet black once) her physique pleasantly plump beneath a bright blue tunic over yellow crepe pants. She's wearing flip-flops trimmed in sequins, and her toes are painted bright red. In her hands is a floral gift bag that Bonnie sets on the counter. "I wanted to say a proper welcome," she says. "I just realized you live right across the hall."

"You didn't know your bestie lives across the hall?" Peter teases. Clara ignores him and asks Bonnie if they've caught the squirrel murderer yet.

Bonnie giggles. Seems to sense the awkwardness between Peter and Clara. "I don't mean to intrude," she finally says, taking a step back toward the still open door. "Wanna go to Tai Chi with me?" she blurts out suddenly.

God no, Clara thinks.

"That would be so good for you," Peter says. "It's some kind of yoga for seniors, right? Supposed to be good for mental health, balance, easy on the joints..."

"Fine, fine," Clara says to shut him up. "But right now I'm really tired. I'm just going to lay down for awhile. You'll take the trash down on your way out, Peter?"

He looks surprised, then hurt, then resigned. "Sure," he says, and stoops to gather the flattened cardboard and plastic bag.

Clara holds the door open a little wider for them both, yawning loudly. "Thanks for stopping by, Bonnie," she says with as much enthusiasm as she can muster. "Bye, honey," she says to Peter and clicks the door closed behind them.

Clara stands for a moment in her unremarkable kitchen and shivers. A faux fur throw on the couch catches her eye. Her brother, Ray, used to tease her about such things. "I could hunt you some rabbits and stitch together a real one," he'd say. "When's the last time you hunted or sewed," she would tease back.

She scoops up the throw on her way to the bedroom, trying not to focus on the out-of-place furniture jammed against one wall, and spreads it over the comforter on her bed. She thinks about her brother's smile. The twinkle in his bright adventure-seeking eyes flashes through her memories then fades away as she wriggles under the covers.

She can't remember going to the mailbox, but she has a letter in her hands. She stands under the pine tree to open it. "It's from my brother," she says to the murdered squirrel; its mouth agape in shock. She unfolds the yellowed stationery to find Ray's familiar lettering. Like their mother, who once won a contest for penmanship, they both share that comforting flowery cursive style. Her stomach settles as she gazes upon a page accented with loopy capital letters and g's that end with a flourish. She can smell the sugar cream pies cooling on her mother's kitchen table where so many letters like this were written.

Dear Dodie, the letter begins.

He's always called me that, she tells the squirrel. When it doesn't laugh, she chuckles, realizing it's only funny to her and Ray.

Sorry I have been remiss in my correspondence. You've been on my mind, as always, though my mind does not always obey my heart or intentions.

It's funny what sticks in our consciences as time marches on. As for me, I cannot shake the image I have of you in our youth. I must have been 9 or 10 years old. You were 2 years younger but so petite and innocent. I can see you peering out the front window, the heavy curtain parted around your elfish face in the corner, watching me ride off on my bike.

I rode my bike far out into the country in those restless days, picking up a stick somewhere along the way and banging it against mailboxes as I counted. I had to ride miles and miles before my stick hit 4 mailboxes. Every time you would beg to come with me, and every time I said "next time."

I didn't have much patience for Mother's wishful-thinking efforts to brighten our futures with useless stuff like piano lessons and all those shopping trips for 'civilized' clothes, as she called it. You were more tolerant than I, helping her bake those pies and selling them so she could 'educate' us out of impoverished futures.

I don't know why, Dodie, but I can't shake that image of you in the window, a mix of disappointment and faith in your eyes. You never doubted I would bring you along. But I never did.

Maybe you are reading this now with no memory of these events. If so, I am thankful. Nevertheless, my neglect sticks in my heart like a rusty nail. You trusted me to make good on my promises, dear sweet little sister. And in the end I proved untrustworthy.

I wish I was the image reflected in your eyes all those years ago. What could have been more important, I can't imagine. But the time for reparation has passed now. And all I can say is I'm sorry. I'm sorry, sweet Dodie. Forgive me or not, but please don't lose that innocent, trustful way you looked upon the world. Please assure me at least I did not steal that from you.
Love always, Raymond.

She is blinded by her tears. They spill onto the beautiful letter from her brother and cause the words to bleed. Blinking, sobbing, Clara wipes her face with her coat sleeves, suddenly concerned she will be noticed. She looks up for the squirrel and finds a blur of beige in its place. She wills her leaden feet to go inside before someone sees her making a spectacle of herself. She can't move. It takes all her strength to turn away from the tree with the squirrel stuck to it.

She wakes to find her pillow damp against her cheek, a dull and soulless bedroom around her, clothes strewn atop unpacked boxes, and an unimpressed pug draped across her feet. Groggily, she wonders how long she napped.

The blinds for her bedroom's window stand open at the sides like sentries, but long shadows stretch across the room. She uncurls her legs from under the covers, alerting Pig who shoots her a glance, snorts and stretches out sleepily. She pads into the bathroom and sees Pig has pooped in the shower. "Sorry Pig," she calls from the toilet. "I guess I slept all day."

She pees, finds some slippers and feels thankful for their warmth. In the kitchen, she sees the pill box and the empty place in the morning row. The noon and evening sections are full. Out of habit, she looks again for the clock above the cabinets that isn't there. She empties the pills remaining for the day into her palm and washes them down with SlimFast. The velvety liquid tastes good. She drinks most of the can, surprised her stomach would hold so much.

In the spare room she surveys the progress. It looks no different than before. She tries not to think about the letter from her brother. Is it even possible he could send her a letter from where he is now, she wonders? The thought stabs at her heart and she pushes it away.

Spotting the scissors on the slim section of desk free from boxes stacked to the ceiling, she plunges them into the box nearest her feet and rips it open.

This one has an assortment of toys she kept in a hand-carved wardrobe back in Florida. The wardrobe stayed behind because it wouldn't fit, she was told. I'd rather have the wardrobe than the toys, she thinks. She bitterly eyes the brightly colored figures in the box.

Peter and his family came to visit her just once after she and Max moved to Florida. She took the grandkids to a movie so Peter and his wife could enjoy a rare night out alone. The boys chose Toy Story. That's why Buzz Lightyear is in the box. When she stopped at Target on the way home and let them pick one toy, they insisted on Buzz.

Their glee was contagious, though Clara has to admit she felt more of an affinity for Woody. He was a good leader. The other toys listened to him. He had no aspirations to venture beyond the good gig he had going in that suburban bedroom. When Buzz came along, Woody's world turned upside down, and after that came nothing but misery. She takes Buzz out of the box. His eyes are dumb and vacant beneath his silly space helmet.

On top of Buzz, she heaps the others one by one. Hulk. A Barbie-like doll but larger. Clara selected that one herself. A Barbie would be dwarfed by the other toys. She wanted the one girl toy to have an even playing field. Next she brings out a snake, long and rubbery, the tongue in its menacing mouth still intact after all these years. She gathers up the newspaper lining the bottom and is surprised to find an army of frogs below the paper. She counts 37 of them as she places each one on the pile over Buzz.

Her grandson, the oldest one, gave her a painting he made of a frog. It was one of the first pictures unpacked, and she made Peter hang it right away. She looks up at it now and relives, as she does every time she sees it, the pride in her grandson's eyes when he handed it to her, the gratefulness she felt for being the one to receive it, his sweet little face watching for her reaction, his delight when she scooped him up and told him how much she loves it. "Are you imprethed with it?" he asked.

All those years ago and seeing a frog still brings it back. The warmth, hope and love. She doesn't remember buying all those frogs, but she must have. Not one of them brings back the feelings that the painting does. She chucks them all back in the box with the other toys, and sets them by the front door.

She notices the gift bag from Bonnie on the counter, peers inside. It's a package of some sort, with paw prints all over it. "It's for you," she says to Pig. He lifts his head and arranges his ears upwards. When she extracts it from the cute floral bag, she sees it is nothing but a bunch of rolled pieces of plastic. On the side, Bonnie has scrawled: "Poop bags. Now you know!" Clara flings the package across the room.

Downstairs, she opens the automatic front doors and unleashes Pig. The wind is blowing crazily. Swirling snowflakes assault Clara's face. Pig looks up at her, bewildered. "Yes, it's cold. Go do your business then. Be quick about it," she says. Clara sets the box of toys down outside for trash pick-up and lets the doors close between them. Pig stays frozen in place with pleading eyes. "Welcome to hell," she says through the glass.

The grassy front yard is flecked grey with snow, dark brooding clouds hovering beyond the street. For a moment, she worries Pig failed to apprehend his mission and will disappear into the icy darkness forever. But back he comes, a little lighter and perkier than before.

"Was that so hard?" she asks once they are in the elevator. He snorts and stares at the numbers, listening for the pings. On Clara's floor, a light flickers as they walk past. She notices for the first time all the pretty wreaths the other tenants have on their doors.

Chapter 3

"I need a wreath," Clara says to Peter before he's through the door, in place of hi how are you.

He removes his boots and sets them in the hallway. "Hi Mom. I love you too." He sniffs and waves his hands in front of his face. "God, Mom. You can't smoke in here, I told you. You're going to get thrown out."

"Good," she says. "I need a wreath. Also I'm going home. I have my car. I hate it here. And that's that."

Peter brings his fists to his eyes and rolls them in the sockets slowly. When he lets his hands fall back to his sides, he looks at Clara, as if he's almost surprised she's still there. He sighs and clears his throat. "Can we have breakfast first?" he asks.

Clara pulls her purse off the counter in a huff. "Be good," she says to Pig. "We'll be back." Pig trots dejectedly over to the couch and sets up camp.

Clara points out the wreaths as they head to the elevator. "Let's take a look at the Dollar Store," Peter says. She tells him about the squirrel as they head toward the lobby. "That's disgusting," Peter says. She starts to ask him if it's true about grey squirrels in Vermont, as they activate the front doors, when she notices the toys.

The box she placed out for trash is gone. No sign of it. But off to the side, Clara notices for the first time a paved patio extending from the front doors to one edge of the building. Lounge chairs and tables have been folded and placed to the side, salt scattered around the paving stones to melt the ice. The patio opens out to the driveway, a thin patch of sod separating the two.

A decorative pillar juts out of the patio's center. The pillar is three feet tall or less. A flat surface on top bears a hole, presumably for an umbrella. Around the pillar, like a minimalist prop on a stage, her toys are arranged. Buzz is out front, pointing back toward the pillar with his right hand. Hulk is facing him defiantly. The girl doll has her hands on her hips, as she peeks around Hulk at Buzz. All 37 frogs hover against the building's edge. The coiled snake peers out from behind the pillar, aiming its venomous fangs toward the frogs.

Clara stops and points, speechless. Peter sees the toy display and says, "That's cute."

"Those are my toys," Clara says.

"You play with toys?" Peter asks.

"Your toys, I mean." Flustered, she adds, "The ones I kept in Florida. In case your kids came to visit."

Peter looks down, ashamed. Clara doesn't feel like talking about squirrels anymore. They drive to the diner in silence.

They open the doors to a tightly packed room bulging with breakfast eaters. One waitress is managing the ten plus tables. Clara sees lobby guy in a booth by the window, and he waves them over.

"This is my son, Peter," she says.

Jimmy introduces himself, which is good, because Clara has already forgotten his name. He invites them to join him. Peter looks impressed Clara has two friends, not just one, so she says ok.

"How did you two meet?" Peter asks.

"A dead squirrel brought us together," Jimmy says, a bit too flirtatiously, Clara thinks.

"What are the odds?" Peter muses. The waitress does a fly by with some menus and says she'll be back. They ask for water and coffee before she can get away.

"Have you seen it yet?" Jimmy asked Peter.

"No, not really that interested in doing so."

"Well, you might be interested in knowing it was a brown squirrel," Clara says. "Bonnie is a Vermonter too and she says the squirrels here are all grey."

"That's true," Peter says, "now that you mention it. We had brown ones in Indiana. Can't say that I've seen brown ones here."

"You guys lived in Indiana?" Jimmy says.

Peter nods. The waitress appears with a tray of waters and cups of coffee. She plunks them down and takes their order. French toast for Clara.

"Regular or real maple syrup?" the waitress asks.

"Real," Jimmy and Peter say for her.

"Trust me," Peter says. "Once you have Vermont maple syrup, you'll never go Aunt Jemima again."

Clara rolls her eyes.

"Flap jacks, real syrup," Jimmy says to the waitress. She scribbles and looks at Peter.

"The Farmer's breakfast," he says. "Bacon, no sausage. Eggs over medium."

The waitress smiles, leaves. Clara looks at Peter with pride. He orders eggs the way she does and knows that bacon trumps sausage.

"I'm from Indiana too," says Jimmy. "Small world." He slurps some coffee. "Squirrels used to migrate, you know."

"Migrate?" Clara asks, stirring two creamers and a stream of sugar into her cup. "Like south for the winter?"

"Like East Coast to Midwest," Jimmy says. "My dad used to say they were so thick in the trees they blocked out the sun for days. I didn't believe him until I saw a swarm of the darned things almost sink a boat."

"That's nuts," Clara says. "Squirrels don't swim."

"Well, they don't migrate anymore either," Jimmy says. "I was canoeing in Wisconsin when I saw a bunch of them darken the lake, hundreds of them, swimming from one end to the other. There was a fishing boat in their path, and they climbed right over it without breaking stride. Darndest thing I've ever seen."

Peter eyes Jimmy over his cup skeptically. "When was that?"

"I'll tell you exactly when," Jimmy says. "1963. I remember because my daughter was born that year, and I didn't canoe in Wisconsin after that. Anyway, I betcha that was the last migration. People say all the clearcutting exposed them to predators on land, including us." He poked a thumb into his own chest. "I guess they adapted and stayed put. Now we have brown ones some places, grey ones in others."

Clara takes a big swallow of her coffee. "Something to say for staying put," she says, glancing at her son. "Soon as I get my car fixed up, I'm going home."

The food arrives, more coffee is requested and delivered, Clara can't believe how good the French toast is and wonders if there's something to the real versus Jemima thing. The three busy themselves with their breakfasts. "Where exactly is home?" Jimmy asks eventually, just as Clara takes a luscious bite of syrupy goodness.

"Exactly," Peter says, stabbing at the home fries on his plate with a fork.

Jimmy looks at Clara, who glares at Peter, swallows, and says, "There are lots of places I can go in Florida."

"Name one," says Peter.

"Liz."

"She's dead."

"Her family, I mean."

"Moved away."

Clara wonders how Peter knows all this, having visited only once. "Juanita," she says.

"Your cleaning lady called me for help getting you to leave. She has a family to feed and you weren't paying rent or expenses."

"That's a fine thank you for employing her all those years, when she couldn't dust the top of a fridge to save her life," Clara says, pushing her plate away.

"I thought Indiana was home," Jimmy offers, in an attempt to defuse the tension.

"Honey, you ever been to Florida?" Clara asks.

"Sure," says Jimmy. "Nice beaches. Not many trees. Lot of alligators. Wouldn't want to be there in the summer." He pretends to wipe sweat from his brow.

Clara considers this for a moment. "The heat isn't a problem when you have air conditioning."

Chapter 4

Cheered by the car's warmth, Clara decides to forgive Peter for his insolence as they drive back to Milton Manor. From the outside, it looks like plain old apartments, three stories high. The apartments along each tier have a sliding glass window, with screens. Clara notices the wrought iron spindles just outside the screens, mimicking a balcony that isn't there. They think we might jump, she thinks, and suddenly wishes she could end herself that easily.

The sun's intensity has melted the patio's skiff of snow. A few smokers soak up the rays, lounging on the now uncovered patio furniture. Peter removes the wreath and small bag of groceries from the car and trails Clara through the front doors. She takes in the toy scene again, sadly. Buzz trying to call the shots. Evil snake lurking around the frogs, and Buzz thinks he's being a hero by directing. He's so oblivious.

"I'll walk Pig for you if you want," Peter says. Clara thanks him, asks if they can walk Pig together. She wants to show him the squirrel.

The same people as always are gathered in the lobby, Jimmy chief among them. They fall silent as Peter and Clara walk by. Jimmy gives them a wave.

They pass the building manager's door on the way to the

mailbox. Peter stops to thank him again for all he did to facilitate his mother's move into the building. "This is my mom right here," he says.

"Hi Clara, I'm Patrick," the man says, stodgily, without getting up.

He is young, she thinks. Reddish hair and freckles. Her son is older than he is, for goodness sakes. Better manners too. "I'm fine thanks," Clara says. "The murdered squirrel though. Makes me wonder what the security in this place is like."

"I beg your pardon?" says Patrick.

Peter interjects with a laugh. "I'm surprised you haven't heard. The whole place is abuzz about a dead squirrel stuck up a tree. We were just about to collect Clara's dog and go have a look."

Patrick's gaze drifts back to his computer as Peter speaks. There's an awkward silence before he looks up again. "You'll find security monitors at every entrance, Clara. I guarantee you safety from … um … squirrels, you said?"

Clara has the distinct impression she is being mocked and she doesn't like it. Before she can challenge young Patrick, Peter says, "Well, we'll leave you to it then." And slips an arm through Clara's, jostling the wreath and groceries to his other arm.

They stop to collect Clara's mail in the lobby. Bonnie is nearby, waiting for the elevator.

"Hey Clara," she chirps. "We're still on for that Tai Chi, right? It's tomorrow at 10."

Clara's in a good mood because of the wreath and doesn't want Peter to see her renege. "Ok. Where is it?"

"It's a 20–30 minute walk from here down the sidewalk. At the Community Center."

"Twenty to thirty minutes," Clara says, punctuating each

syllable. "Who exercises on the way to exercise? Tell you what, I'll drive."

"Great," Bonnie says. She looks at Peter for confirmation. Peter is shuffling through the mail, sorting the bills from the junk.

Clara has to admit she is a little surprised Pig didn't poop in the shower today. They'd been gone over half the day, and she had rushed him out the main doors again that morning to do his business so she wouldn't have to walk on the ice. He wastes no time doing his business, however, under the pine tree.

Peter can't explain the squirrel's predicament either. How does an agile, expert climber and jumper (supposed swimmer, even) manage to land against a tree trunk, claws out rather than in? And what kind of rotten luck would it have to have to additionally impale itself on some strong kind of twig growing out of the trunk?

"Exactly," Clara says. "Someone murdered it."

"Or some thing," Peter teases. An eerie shadow of the squirrel stretches down the trunk. "What are those whitish bits on the squirrel?" Peter asks, squinting.

Clara studies the squirrel for a few moments and doesn't see it at first. "Oh, ugh!" she says. "Something's been eating it."

"What?"

"Those aren't white bits, they're pink. Something's been taking bites out of it." Clara turns away in disgust and tugs Pig along with her.

"Wait, Mom. What about the poop?"

"Did he poop? I don't see anything."

Peter rolls his eyes. "You didn't bring out any bags, did you? Mom, they're going to throw you out. You have to follow the rules." Peter runs his hand through his hair and seems to make his breathing more purposeful. "Do you understand, Mom? There's no room at my place, and the next step on your budget is a full on government-funded nursing home, with dying roommates all around you."

"Whatever. Once the car is fixed up, I'm out."

They walk back toward the garage. A man Clara hasn't met passes by them on the way. Something about the way he looks at her, wordlessly, gives her the creeps. She shudders, and Peter puts his arm around her.

"I love you, Mom," he says. "You're a royal pain in my behind, but I love you. Did it ever occur to you that I want you here for my sake? That I want to be near you?"

"I'm dying here though," Clara says, patting his hand on her shoulder. "It's not my home, and I hate it."

They walk to her apartment in silence the rest of the way. Peter picks up the pile of bills and notices the package of poop bags on the floor in front of the TV. He walks over and picks it up, puts it on the coffee table. Pig watches from his perch on the couch, and Peter stoops to pat his head. "I'd hate to see you lose this guy," Peter says.

Clara pretends she doesn't hear this. She is old and tired and even she wonders at times if Pig deserves better. But she lost her dad, her mom, her life love Max, and after that the pain in her heart iced over into something she cannot name. Pig is the only being in the world left who loves her unconditionally.

"This is strange," Peter says, extracting one envelope from the pile of bills he means to bring home.

"What?" says Clara. "I haven't put a thing on my credit card, like you said. I still have $100 of the cash you got out for me."

"No, it's not a bill. It's from the building manager."

"Patrick?"

Peter looks up from the letter. "It says you aren't picking up the poop. That you've been asked to do it, and you blatantly refused."

Bonnie! Clara thinks, seeing red.

"They have you on security cameras letting Pig out off leash in the no-pets area out front."

Clara sits down next to Pig on the couch and lets the TV's scrolling news-line hypnotize her, take her to another place. She hates it here.

Peter finishes reading and places the letter on the counter. "At least they didn't mention your smoking in the apartment," he says, kissing her on the top of the head and letting himself out.

Clara takes a pack out from the decorative vase on the coffee table in front of her, shakes out a cigarette, digs out the lighter from under her cushion and has herself a good, calming smoke.

Chapter 5

Clara picks up the letter Peter left on the counter. After she had her cigarette and opened the windows to air out the place, she had gone to the bathroom easily (one of the things she likes about smoking) and had herself a peaceful sleep. She doesn't remember waking up exactly. The morning sunlight pours through the window. She swallows her pills from the AM row with a swig of SlimFast, sees the letter, and resolves to get it over with. She sprays a little Febreze first and notices it's not working. She jots down a note to get some more and starts to read.

My Dear Clara, it begins.

That's rather informal she thinks. Then again, she did find Patrick unmannerly. Her opinion of him and his management style could not be any lower.

You probably feel guilty for pulling the plug. We did talk about it though and you were absolutely right. I was very clear about my insistence about being allowed to die without tubes and what-not all around and in me if it came to that.

Wow, Clara thinks. Patrick is more of an idiot than I thought. He switched out my letter for another tenant's mail somehow. Well, I might as well finish reading it now that I've started.

And I saw the look in your eyes the day before I had the second heart attack. I was getting stronger, and you chastised me for trying to get up and walk around even though the doctors told me to rest. I felt so good and I thought I had a new lease on life. I promised you the best sex of your life as soon the hospital released me, and you tried to be happy for me.

I realize now you were likely thinking about how hard it had been for you those last few years watching me slowly suffocate from emphysema. I was a shadow of my former self. I was helpless and I hated it. The worst part was watching you grow weary of it too. So when the doctors offered surgery as an option for extending my quality of life a little longer, I was happy to see you embracing the news right along with me. We were going to get another chance, if all went well, to go back to our beautiful life together, if even for a few months, before my lungs would start to fail me again.

Neither of us could have predicted the second heart attack, my love. So I'm writing to release you of whatever guilt or regret you might harbor inside. I know you must *wonder if you were doing what I truly wished when you signed the DNR order. We were fooling ourselves, thinking we could cheat life into giving us more time.*

You had no idea when you married me that the 20 years between us would land us in that predicament. It crossed my mind but I was too selfish to realize I couldn't will myself to stay healthy at the same rate as your youth. My hope is that you have moved on, that you have found a joy that keeps you buoyant in the world the way you buoyed me up while I was a part of it. Forgive me, dear Clara, for being too old to love you long enough.

Love always, Max.

"No!" screams Clara, dropping the letter. This isn't a Patrick mix-up. It's another dream letter. Why another one? Oh, wake up, wake up, Clara. This one is even more painful than the last.

As the world reforms back around her, she sees that the sun is not streaming through the window. It's nighttime still, and snowflakes are streaming from the heavens like the tears on her pillow. She gathers up Pig, asleep at her feet, and hugs him close. "I love you, Pig," she says, great big sobs heaving her chest in painful waves. "You're all I have left."

At the first sign of light, Clara, picks up her purse and makes sure her wallet is in it, her keys and her phone. She considers the pill box, but it's too big. She opens all the slots and pours them out into her purse. Next she snaps the leash on to Pig, his toes already doing a dance on the linoleum beside her. She takes him to the pine, snow crunching underfoot, and let's him sniff around while she checks out the squirrel. Its grotesqueness is unspeakable. Half its torso is missing now. Pig is kicking snow up with his back legs, signalling he is done and she carefully steps over all the other poo piles on her way to the car. She takes out her keys and instantly finds the right one. Funny, she has to try every key on her ring to unlock her apartment door or the mailbox, but she hasn't forgotten her car key. It's a powerful symbol for her, her ticket to freedom.

She sits inside for a few moments, Pig panting expectantly in the passenger seat beside her. The thought of her baby sister comes to her without warning. She has not allowed herself to think of Sophie in years, how she was found in the garage, car running, squelching out her life for no reason anyone could discern. It was Clara's first real loss. Sophie was more than a sister. She was her first best friend. The abandonment Clara felt in the wake of her suicide was barely tolerable. She drifted through the next few years of her life like a ghost, friendless and confused. But she had her Max back then. Her parents were more destroyed than she was. "Parents die before children. Not the other way around," they kept saying. But at least she had them too. She even had her brother, though he was preoccupied with his own family during that time and not much comfort beyond the general sense of belongingness his presence in the world provided.

She thinks of her mother, dying slowly in that abysmal nursing home. Her mother was ready, having lost a child, her husband, her siblings. "Why won't my body die?" she kept asking Clara. What is death really, Clara thinks, other than the slow snuffing out of every person you love. After all that roots you to this world is gone, surely that's a spiritual kind of death the body has no choice but to follow.

This is the thing Peter does not understand. He has a wife, two able sons wrapped up in their own careers. His father is gone, true. Clara remembers her first husband more fondly now that he has beaten her to the grave. But Peter has a whole life here still. He can't comprehend the loss, the deep darkness of too much love snatched away. Peter moved her here to solve a math equation. She must forgive him for failing to see the spiritual death she began back in Florida was her prerogative, not his. She can't live out her last few breaths in a foreign place she despises, and that despises her. Whatever the risks, she has to go back to the last place she identified as home. The place where she sensed community all around her. A brown squirrel belongs with other brown squirrels.

Pig has curled up next to her. "Sorry Pig," she says. "I needed a minute." She inserts the key and twists.

Chapter 6

Two things occur to Clara, as she tries to start the car again. One, the car is dead. Two, there is snow all over it, and she does not own a snow brush.

She walks back into Milton Manor through the front doors. The snow has transformed the toy scene into an assortment of little ghost lumps. Jimmy and his gaggle of gossipers are sipping coffee in the lobby. "Let me get that door for you," Jimmy calls out, without moving.

"Ha, ha," Clara mock-laughs back.

The manager's door is open so she and Pig waltz right in. "You're not Patrick," Clara says, eyeing the spectacle of a person in Patrick's chair.

"Cute dog," says the spectacle. The spectacle rises to shake Clara's hand. She (no, wait, Clara thinks, maybe 'he') is blue. Long denim shirt over aqua skinny pants, navy sneakers, short cropped hair dyed blue, and a face with unremarkable features except for the mouth twisted into a tentative smile. "I'm Radish," the spectacle says.

"What kind of name is Radish?" Clara asks.

Radish bends down and offers Pig her hand. He sniffs and snorts his approval. She cups his ears in her hands and massages his head. He melts into the massage, arcing his whole body around her stooped knees. "Yiddish," Radish says.

"Yiddish," Clara repeats.

"Kidding." Radish stands again, and Clara sees she is quite tall. And thin. "My parents are a bit hippy dippy."

"Is Patrick gone?" Clara asks hopefully. Not that she plans to stick around, but she would rather deal with the spectacle than Patrick the mannerless dolt.

"Nope. He had a commitment today. I just fill in at nights around here and days when Patrick is off. I live here, actually."

"In a seniors home? What are you, nine? Isn't that against the rules?"

Radish laughs. "Actually no. It was the only place available that met my needs. And like I said, I work here too. So..." Radish walks back over to her desk. "...what can I do for you?"

Pig strains at the leash to follow Radish. Clara tells him to sit and gives his head a pat. "I need a snow brush. And a jump start."

"Oof," says Radish. "I can lend you my snow brush, but I don't have any jumper cables. Suppose you could call the garage in town and see if they can jump your car or tow it somewhere." She jots down a number on a Post-it and hands it across the desk to Clara. "Or I could give you a lift if you like?"

"Only if you're going to Florida."

"Sadly, no," Radish says. She neither asks why Clara would be going to Florida nor furrows her brow at the prospect of a woman her age intending to do such a thing.

So Clara exhales the breath she didn't know she was holding in. "Thanks anyway."

She hears a swelling of laughter in the lobby and gets an idea. "Jimmy," she says, walking straight into the gossip circle and planting herself on an empty orange chair closest to him. Pig sits in front of her, facing the others defensively, his neck shackles stiffening. She glances quickly at the silent seniors whose good time she has interrupted. "I need a jump start. You have a car, right?"

"Nice of you to join us," Jimmy says. "Allow me to introduce you. This is Hugh..." He points to a transplanted farmer type in overalls to his left. "...Millie..." he continues, referencing the dumpy curly headed woman next to Hugh... Blah, blah, blah is all Clara hears after that. Finally, he finishes with, "... and this is my friend, Clara."

"Hi Clara," they say in monotone unison.

"Hi," Clara says, mentally fixating for some reason on the word friend. She smiles weakly at the assembly she cares not to know and turns back to Jimmy. "Pardon my interruption, and I am pleased to make your acquaintance..." she throws over her shoulder to the court. "...but would you be so kind as to give my car a jump start? Kind sir."

"There you are," sings Bonnie, "I've been looking all over for you." Into the lobby she marches, wearing some kind of catsuit looking outfit meant for exercising younger bodies, and brimming with enthusiasm. "You didn't forget, did you? Is that what you're wearing to Tai Chi?"

Not the goddam Tai Chi, Clara thinks. She is still wearing what she slept in, she realizes. Tentatively, Clara brings her hand up to the buttons on her pea coat and thinks yes she's wearing a bra at least. But no way is she going to Tai Chi. "You ratted me out to Patrick," Clara blurts.

Bonnie stands at the edge of the lobby, mouth open, noting the gossip circle turned her way.

"You're always on at me about 'pick up the poop, pick up

the poop, did you pick up the poop, HERE you go, HERE is a whole package of poop bags so you can pick up the goddam POOP,'" Clara rants. "And now I have a letter from management accusing me of ... wanna take a guess?"

"Not picking up the poop," the court mumbles in unison.

"Thank you," Clara says to the gossip circle and turns back to Bonnie.

Bonnie's cheeks turn pink. She closes her mouth, takes a deep breath in as if to steel herself for what comes next. "I did not rat you out," she finally says in the quietest sing song-y whisper Clara has ever heard, "but I know who did." There is a quick inhale of breath amongst the court. "Now, are you coming to Tai Chi. Or not?"

"Absolutely," says Jimmy. "I'll drive."

Chapter 7

Jimmy from Indiana drives a Kia. Does that even make sense, Clara wonders. She is smushed into the back seat, clutching the poop bag package Jimmy insisted that she bring, Pig panting next to her happily. Bonnie has shotgun so she can give Jimmy directions. Clara would have (should have, she thinks) said absolutely no to Tai Chi. But alas, Jimmy is her easiest and, let's face it, cheapest ticket to a jump start, so it's best for now to humor him. Also, Bonnie refuses to tell her who the resident rat is, and Clara figures one Tai Chi class is a small price to pay for a little information.

"Turn left at the light," Bonnie directs.

"Who's the rat?" Clara asks.

Bonnie and Jimmy exchange a look. "OK get in the right lane because you are going to turn there after Kinney's Drug Store," Bonnie says.

"Who's the rat?" Clara asks.

"You're going to drive straight until the road comes to a T. And turn right."

"Holy Hell," Clara says. "You wanted to walk all this way? Who's the rat?"

Bonnie huffs and turns to Clara in the back seat. "I'm not going to tell you until you stop being mean."

"Mean?" Clara exclaims incredulously. "I am not mean. Vermonters are mean. I don't gossip, I use my manners, and I keep to myself. That's not mean. That's dignified."

"Manners?" Bonnie says. "Yes, turn right here," she directs Jimmy, "the community center is on the left just there, see?"

Jimmy nods. "Got it."

"What is so polite about not answering when people speak to you?" Bonnie says to Clara. "What is polite about ranting at a person who's supposed to be your best friend in front of a crowd? What is polite about assuming a person is your best friend without asking her first if she even likes you?"

"You like everyone," Clara says.

"I don't like you. You're mean," Bonnie says.

Clara rolls her eyes. "Fine. Don't tell me who the rat is. It's probably you anyway, and this is just a big whoop-de-doo to distract me from the truth."

Jimmy parks, and Bonnie opens the door. She gets out, stands up, then leans back in. "See?" she says to Clara. "Mean."

Clara sighs and opens her door. "Thank you, Jimmy, for the drive," she says, hoping for some jump start bonus points. "And for walking Pig. Not that I asked you to do that. He doesn't like exercise much."

"And for picking up his poop?" he says, reaching for the poop bag package.

She hands it to him and gives him a fake smile.

"See you guys back here in 30 minutes," Jimmy says, and Clara saunters toward the glass doors she saw Bonnie enter.

The class is excruciating. And by that, Clara means boring, not hard or painful. The class is comprised of four people, including her and Bonnie, excluding the teacher. One is a double amputee in a wheelchair, and the other is a skinny old waif in a jump suit circa Gene Simmons. They sit in a circle of chairs and make flowing motions with their arms that the teacher seems to be learning himself, reading from his notes.

"So this isn't the thing I see in the parks that looks like a cross between yoga and exotic dancing?" Clara asks.

"Yes, that is Tai Chi. Very good, Clara," says Rob the teacher. "This is the same thing, but in chairs. Research shows tremendous improvements in balance for seniors who practice Tai Chi. We start off in chairs to learn the principals in baby steps. We are so fortunate to have the funding here to offer chair Tai Chi for free this session. If there's enough interest, we will offer beginners Tai Chi next session," Rob says enthusiastically, his beer belly rippling with the last flourish of his spaghetti arm movements.

"So no chairs next session?" asks Clara imitating the flourish with one limp wrist.

"Beginners is in chairs too," Rob says excitedly.

Clara raises her eyebrows at Bonnie, who gives Clara a don't-be-mean look.

Afterwards, Clara is exhausted from pretending to participate. Bonnie is bouncing off the walls with energy. "That was grrrr-eat!" she enthuses.

"Easy there, Tiger," Clara says. "You might bruise a joint if you aren't careful." They spot the Kia across the parking lot, with Jimmy and Pig in front of it, Pig sniffing at the shrubbery.

"How'd it go?" Clara asks Jimmy, when they get closer. Pig waggles up to her, all atwitter with energy. She eyes him suspiciously. "Did you give him cat nip or something?"

"Ha!" says Jimmy. "Just a vigorous walk in the woods. There's a path over there." He points to a clump of trees behind the Community Centre. "Pig loves the trees."

"Wonders never cease," Clara says, play sparring with Pig as he snorts and dances in front of her. She can't help but smile for real. The class was horrendous, but the company isn't bad. She aims her smile at Bonnie, as they all pile into the Kia.

Bonnie smiles back and pats Clara's knee. "That was fun," Bonnie says.

"Who's the rat?" Clara asks. "Kidding," she says quickly, before Bonnie's frown can take up residence on her face. "You don't have to tell me. It doesn't matter anyway. I'm going back to Florida. Jimmy? If it's not too much trouble, would you give me a jump start when we get back?"

"I'd love to, he says, but I don't have any cables." He sees Clara's disappointment in the rear-view mirror. "Do you have a place to stay when you get there?"

Clara thinks through the conversation from the diner with Peter and can't honestly say yes. But she also can't stay in a place where she doesn't belong and therefore has no choice. Surely, Juanita will take her in if she's polite about it. Maybe she'll offer to do a little dusting for her. She has a bit of money and a debit card. That should buy her some time while she works out where she is meant to be in Florida at this stage in her life. "I'll figure it out," she finally says to Jimmy.

They drive in silence the rest of the way. They have to rouse Pig from a full on snooze-fest to get him out of the car. Someone has shovelled the snow on the patio, but the furniture is gone now. It's the clearest sign Clara can think of that winter has arrived.

The toys have been brushed off and rearranged. The snake is out in front of the rocks, as if looking for different prey. Buzz and Hulk are either wrestling or hugging, Clara can't tell for sure. And the frogs are crowded around the girl doll in the corner. She has her hands held up high like she's singing, or conducting a symphony, or maybe it's a stiff armed doll version of Tai Chi.

There are no gossipers in the lobby when they come through the doors. Jimmy walks over to his usual chair near the window and sits down. Clara does the same, on a couch opposite the windows. She doesn't want to go back to her apartment just yet, and this is the first time the lobby has been vacant and inviting. Pig waits at the end of the leash and stares off at Bonnie, who is loitering by the doors.

"You wanna join us, bestie?" Clara asks.

Bonnie laughs and seats herself in the orange chair near Jimmy. Pig leaps onto the chair next to Clara and eyes the three of them sleepily.

Clara is still tired from the class but wishes to avoid her usual afternoon nap. "I get letters in my dreams," she says without intending to say it outside her head.

"What kind of letters?" Jimmy asks.

Clara looks him in the eyes, not sure if she can be honest. She'd rather keep Jimmy at arm's length, their sardonic bantering provides levity and structure to her days. His eyes are kind, though, and she decides to risk it. "Painful ones. From people I love who left me forever."

"Are they mean?" Bonnie asks.

Clara thinks about what mean is, then laughs to herself when she thinks mean is meaningless. It's just one person's perspective on what offends or hurts another person, she decides. "Yes and no," she says. "They dredge up experiences I'd rather not remember."

Jimmy says, "Sounds cheaper than therapy."

Clara smiles. "Therapy is for wimps."

"I paint dreams," Bonnie offers. "Well, not dreams per se, but scenes that happen behind my eyelids."

Jimmy and Clara turn toward Bonnie, their faces puzzled.

"When I close my eyes," Bonnie says, "and focus – really focus on the backs of my eyelids – I see patterns. I always have."

"What kind of patterns?" Clara asks.

"Depends. There are some repeating ones. Orange background with brown tree branch type engravings over it is typical. It's a treat when I get purple or red or bright green colors. The patterns grow and shrink, so I can never nail it exactly. A couple of times I've had fireworks — splashes of vibrant colors erupting in front of me one after another. I've tried to keep the scenes going, and I've tried to make them stop, but I can't control them. They come from someplace outside of me. One day I decided to paint them as best I can, and that makes me happy."

"I get dream letters, and Bonnie gets eyelid art. What's your disability?" Clara asks Jimmy.

"Special gift," corrects Bonnie.

Jimmy thinks for a moment. "Not sure if I have one. Does a Kia count?"

"No," Bonnie and Clara say in unison.

Just then, Radish appears, heading for the front doors.

"Radish," Clara calls to her. "Come meet my friends." Again she feels a fixation with the word friends. It's losing its plastic quality.

"Oh hi there!" Radish says, waving her blue arm about. "I'll be back. Just heading out to grab lunch."

Bonnie and Jimmy introduce themselves quickly and ask who she is here visiting.

"Oh I live here," she says. "And I work here sometimes, filling in for Patrick."

Since Bonnie and Jimmy are speechless, Clara chimes in, "Can you believe that? I mean..." she turns to Radish, "...you can't be older than 15?"

"18. To make a long, very boring story short, my parents moved to Vancouver, I wanted to stay here and finish high school, and this is the only place in my school district that had a room to rent."

"That must be expensive," Jimmy says.

"I get a discount for filling in for the manager. And I work at McDonalds. Listen, guys, I gotta motor but I'll be back soon, ok? Nice to see you, Jimmy. Nice to meet you, Bonnie." And out she goes.

The three of them look at each other with wide eyes. Pig snores and stretches his legs further out on the couch.

"What a nice fellow," Jimmy finally says.

"Girl you mean," says Bonnie.

They look at Clara for confirmation. "Don't look at me," says Clara. "Whatever she is, I like him. This place needs a little injection from the young. Speaking of, who do you think is making the toy scenes out front on the patio?"

"I don't know," Jimmy says. "I see Willie out there once in awhile, but lots of people go out to smoke."

"I can't imagine Willie being that playful," Bonnie says.

"Who's Willie?" Clara asks.

"Willie Wedge. War vet," Jimmy says. "He's a bit off, but not too bad when you get to know him. He comes to the bingo games from time to time."

"What does he look like?" Clara asks.

Jimmy and Bonnie look at each other as they try to think of a description.

"Dark clothes?" Bonnie offers.

"Camo," Jimmy adds.

"Medium height, quiet. Actually," Bonnie whispers, leaning in, "he's the one I think ratted you out, Clara."

"What? Why?"

"He smokes," Bonnie says. "He sees all the poop while he's out there and gets mad about it. I've heard him make comments."

"I can't be the only one who forgets to pick up poop once in awhile," Clara says. Jimmy and Bonnie roll their eyes. "Surely you don't smoke," Clara says to Bonnie. "What are you doing out there with the smokers?"

Bonnie shrugs. "There was a lot of drama about the squirrel. I found it entertaining. It's gross now though."

"Who do people think killed it?" Clara asks.

"Oh you're the only one who thinks that," says Bonnie. "Most people think it was an accident. There is a theory that the grey squirrels ganged up on it and managed to get it to kill itself."

"Baloney," Clara says.

"Seriously. There are studies, I guess, that prove squirrels are territorial. If you catch one and release it somewhere else, it will find its way back. Why? Because the new squirrel community will reject it."

"That's sad," Clara says.

"Yes, I agree. I guess they are territorial. AND brown squirrels are more aggressive than grey ones, so maybe the crucified squirrel tried to bully his way in," Bonnie says with a gleam in her eye. "Willie's the one with the territorial theory by the way."

"Well, he sounds like quite the charmer," Clara says. "I can't wait to meet him." She glances at Jimmy, who has gone quiet all of a sudden. He is staring at the window. The sun is out and the untouched snow on the lawn across the driveway sparkles. "Tired, Jimmy?"

"No, I was just thinking," he says. "I'm in the mood for adventure. What if the three of us road trip to Florida? I'll drive."

Chapter 8

When Clara wakes up from her nap, the daylight pervades her living area, which she finds encouraging. Pig is at the door, doing his linoleum dance, as she looks over her pill box. It's empty. Someone has stolen her pills, she thinks. She gets her purse, takes out her phone, and turns it on. Peter picks up on the first ring.

"Are you okay, Mom?" he asks.

"Someone stole my pills," she says.

"That's not good. How long has it been since you've had your medication?"

"How would I know? There's no clock in my kitchen and the AM, noon, and PM rows are all empty," Clara says, exasperated.

"Ok, think now. What have you done today? What did you do when you woke up?"

"Well, I got up and read the letter from Patrick, only it wasn't from Patrick, it was from Max, and then I...Wait. That was a dream." Clara's mind goes blank. She trembles, places a hand on the kitchen counter to brace herself.

"I'll be right over."

Dance, dance, Pig's feet say.

"What has gotten into you?" Clara asks. She checks the shower for poop and finds none. "Good boy," she says, and snaps on his leash. They pad down the hallway, get into the elevator, and ride it to the garage level. She walks Pig out the open garage door and across the parking lot to the smoking area. Jimmy is there smoking.

"Have you seen my pills?" Clara asks.

Jimmy exhales and shakes his head. "I don't think so. You ok?"

"Well, I'll be ok when I find the thief who took my pills." Pig takes a massive dump next to the pine tree, and Clara looks up out of habit. The squirrel is gone. A guilty looking stub of a twig remains. And a giant red X has been painted on the trunk. "What's that all about?" Clara says, pointing to the X.

"I guess the tree is unhealthy," Jimmy says. "They've marked it for destruction."

They take in the tree, it's broad fragrant branches, and the shelter underneath that blocks the wind. "Because of the squirrel?" Clara asks.

"I don't think so," Jimmy says. He roots around in his jacket pocket. He has on his jeans with holes and baseball cap but is wearing a puffy coat. "Here," he says, and hands Clara a poop bag. "I kept a few from my walk with Pig."

"Thanks." She bends down to scoop Pig's poop. The memory comes at her in a rush. "You walked Pig, I went to Tai Chi. That's what I did today. That's why Pig is so dance-y. He's still all revved up from the walk."

"Sounds about right," Jimmy says with a chuckle. "You sure you're ok?"

"I'm fine," she says, relieved. "Peter asked me what I did this morning, and my mind went blank."

"That's too bad," Jimmy says.

Clara narrows her eyes at Jimmy. "What's going on with you? You're not acting yourself."

"How would you know what my self looks like?" Jimmy says back.

Clara thinks she should have an answer but can't come up with one.

"I'm sorry," he says. "I'm just distracted. There have been some rumors flying about this place, and I let them get to me is all."

"Gossiping is bad," Clara says. "I hate this place."

"I know you do."

"Well?" Clara says, holding up the bag at arms length between them.

"Over there, just inside the garage. There's a door on your left. You'll find a dumpster in there." He stubs out his cigarette and walks over to the picnic table under the rickety little shelter set up for smokers and throws his butt into a can there.

"Thanks." Clara heads back to the garage and finds the door Jimmy told her about. The door is heavy, and she struggles to hold it open for Pig. Pig refuses to go in, and she sees there is a stopper at the bottom of the door she can press down with her foot to keep the door ajar.

"Stay," she says, and drops the leash. She sees two dumpsters. One says recycling and one doesn't. She opens the top of the one that doesn't and throws the poop in it. That's not so bad, she thinks. She hears a car starting up as she turns to leave and sees that Pig is not where she told him to stay. She rushes out of the dumpster room just as a car comes screeching toward her. Pig is between her and the car, and at the last minute he scuffles out of the way in between two parked cars.

Clara ducks back into to the dumpster room, hears the wheels squealing to avoid the still open door and looks out as the car exits the garage. In the front seat is a darkly clothed man with a camo cap.

Chapter 9

Clara is sobbing and hugging Pig with all her strength when she gets back to her apartment. Peter is inside already, searching the floor near her pillbox. Before he can ask, she blurts, "Someone tried to kill Pig."

Peter takes Pig out of her arms and sets him on the floor, watches him run over to the sofa and curl up on the blanket there. "Here have some water," Peter says, and takes a clean glass out of the cabinet, fills it with water and hands it to Clara.

She drinks in rushed gulps, takes a big breath in between, and drinks some more. She sticks out her tongue. "I hate water."

"OK listen. Can you calm down and tell me what happened now?"

Clara tries to think, but it all comes back to her in a blur. "I was talking to Jimmy."

"Where?"

"By the dead squirrel. But there's no dead squirrel now. He had a poop bag for me. He told me where to throw it away. When I came out, someone was trying to run over Pig."

"Run over how?" Peter says.

"With his car!" she screams. "What do you think?"

"OK. You said his. Was it a man you recognized?"

"No. Yes. I don't know. He was creepy." She looks up at

Peter suddenly. "Like the guy we passed that time. When I showed you the squirrel. He looked a lot like that guy."

"Did anyone else see this?" asks Peter. "What about Jimmy? Was he still out by the squirrel tree?"

"I don't think so. I wasn't really looking. After he sped off, I went to find Pig. He was shaking and trying to hide."

Peter sighs. "OK. We should go talk to Patrick about this. Meanwhile, I've brought some medicine for you." He lines up four pill bottles on the counter. "Did you take your morning pills?"

Clara thinks back but doesn't know.

"Well, I'll give you your noon pills then. And keep an eye on you for awhile." He hands them to her with a glass of water.

"I hate water."

"Fine." He shakes a half empty can of SlimFast at her. "How long has this been around?"

"I don't know." She takes it from him, puts the pills in her mouth, and drinks the rest of the can.

Clara sits on the couch and watches the scroll of news creep across the bottom of the TV screen.

"Why do you watch this all day?" Peter asks.

"I like FOX News," she says.

"Do you ever change the channel?"

"To what?"

Peter rolls his eyes and switches the station. The bell rings. Pig looks up but doesn't bark or move. "Hi Bonnie," Peter says, letting her in.

"Oh hi Peter," Bonnie says. "I didn't know you were here. I can come back later."

"Actually, do you mind staying? Mom's not quite herself."

"Oh sure."

Bonnie has on a floral muumuu with jewelled flip flops. Clara can't remember why she expects her to be wearing a black catsuit.

"How was your nap?" Bonnie says, sitting in the lounge chair by the couch. "Get any letters?" she says with an exaggerated wink.

"I don't think so, Bonnie. Did you take my pills?"

"What pills?"

"I have pills that go in that very dainty pill box over there." She gestures to the kitchen bar. "Peter fills it up for me. It was empty when I woke up from my nap."

"Hmmm. Did you lock your door when we went to Tai Chi?"

"You went to Tai Chi?" Peter asks.

"I went to Tai Chi," Clara exclaims. "That's why you should be wearing a catsuit."

Bonnie furrows her brow, looks at Peter, then at Clara. "So Jimmy made you come up here for the poop bags before we left. Were the pills here then?" Bonnie says.

"I don't remember," Clara says, sadly.

"Do you remember if you locked the door?"

"Do you think Jimmy took my pills?" she asks Bonnie incredulously.

"I think we are getting off track here," Peter says. To Bonnie, he adds, "She's not herself. She missed at least one dose of her medication. That's why she's confused."

"And someone tried to run over Pig. That's pretty goddam confusing," Clara adds, with frustration in her voice.

"Someone what?" Bonnie says.

"And Jimmy's acting weird," Clara says, instead of answering. "Do you know what's wrong with him?"

Bonnie looks at Peter for help. He shrugs.

"Tell you what," Clara says, with surprising clarity to Bonnie. "You go find Jimmy and ask him why he's acting so weird. You," she says to Peter, "go find Patrick the young dolt boy and tell him to put his goddam security cameras to use looking for that dog-killing bad guy instead of wasting his pathetic excuse for a life tracking down poop violators." Clara lets out an exasperated sigh.

Bonnie shrugs this time. "Ok."

"You'll be okay by yourself?" Peter asks. Clara glares at him in response. "Right. On my way then. Don't forget there's an emergency button in the bathroom," he says.

"Go," she says.

"I'll lock the door on the way out," he says, rooting around in her purse for the keys. "Oh...I think I found the missing pills."

Chapter 10

When Clara wakes up, Pig is not at her feet. She uses the bathroom and checks the shower. All good there, she thinks. She pads into the kitchen, and checks the pill box. All slots are full, so she shakes out the morning pills. She looks around for her SlimFast. Opens the fridge. Cracks open a new one. Puts the pills in her mouth and swallows. She takes two more big sips and sets the can on the bar next to her pill box.

The TV is off, which is strange, because it's always on. Then she sees Peter sleeping on the couch, Pig stretched out over his feet. His stubby little tail wags tentatively when she sees him. "There's my good boy," she says, and he slides off the couch to greet her. He waggles and starts his linoleum dance as she freshens his water and puts food in his dish.

Peter wakes up and offers to walk Pig.

"Yes. Please," Clara says. "Why did you sleep here? Marital discord back at home?" she teases.

"You're back to your old self," Peter says, stretching his arms, then his back, before standing up. "You were confused yesterday, and I was worried about you."

"I like having you here."

"Well, stop the presses. We're going to want that in writing," Peter jokes. He is still wearing jeans and a flannel shirt. He opens the closet and grabs his parka. Snaps on Pig's leash. Clara is just staring at him. She feels grateful for the smile that comes so easily, the warmth spreading through her chest that's almost but not quite an ache. "What?" he says.

She gives him a big hug. He hugs her back and lets her hang on as long as she wants. "I'll make you coffee," she says.

"I'll have an egg over medium too," he says, winking, and trails Pig out the door.

When he comes back, Bonnie is sitting on the couch as Clara folds up the blankets. There is a steaming cup of coffee on the bar.

"Good morning, Bonnie," he says and opens the cabinet under the sink.

"What do you think you're doing?" Clara says.

Throwing out the poop.

"Not there you don't," Clara says. "In the dumpster. Elevator to the basement. Door on the right just before the big open exit. Pick a dumpster. Throw it in."

Peter looks at her blankly. "You're serious," he finally says.

Bonnie shrugs. Clara says nothing.

"Fine," he says and leaves.

"So they say he's on a sexual predator list or whatever," Bonnie says, after Peter leaves.

"Jimmy's no predator," Clara says.

"I know. I mean, how would we know for sure? I'm just telling you what people are saying. You asked me to find out why he's not acting himself, and that's what I found out."

"Did you ask HIM why he's not acting himself?" Clara asks.

"I couldn't find him. Anyway, you said he mentioned

something about rumors. So there you go. That must be the rumor that was bugging him."

"Well, it can't be true," Clara says. "He's nice."

Bonnie gives her a half smirk.

"Fine," Clara says. "But rumors are bad. Nothing good ever comes from them. I'm going to tell the building manager to put an end to them."

"Fine," says Bonnie.

"Fine," says Clara.

"So," Bonnie whispers, eyeing the door for Peter's return. "You ready for our road trip?"

"Can't wait to get out of here," Clara says. "It's tomorrow right?"

"Day after," says Bonnie. "Hope all this predator talk doesn't lose us a driver."

"Where are you driving?" Peter says, giving Pig some love at the door.

Bonnie's eyes widen and lock with Clara's. "Nowhere," Clara says. "Because my car won't start. Can you give me a jump, Peter?"

Peter eyes her suspiciously. "So you can drive where?"

"Radish works at McDonald's. I love McDonald's. I would like to be able to drive there sometimes to go see her," Clara says. Then with a decisive nod aimed in Bonnie's direction, she adds, "And get a cheeseburger."

Peter takes a sip of his coffee. "Since when do you eat something besides SlimFast and French toast?"

"Ha. Ha," Clara says. "I also drink Pepsi."

"And who is Radish?"

"Oh! She's...or he's...we're not quite sure, a fill-in for Patrick. She lives here."

"Uh. Huh," Peter says. "Well, I do have to get back. It looks like you are in good hands here. Thank you, Bonnie." Peter gives her a dramatic bow. "I'll take a look at your car on my way out and see what I can do."

"Wait," Clara says. She gets up and roots around in her purse, then opens the closet and checks her peacoat pockets. "Here it is." She hands him a Post-it. "Radish gave me the number of a garage in Milton. If you can't jump it, can you get it towed to the garage?"

Peter looks at the Post-it and shakes his head. Sighs. "I guess you are not going to let this go until I do."

"Thank you," she says. Gives him a hug.

Peter casts a bewildered look in Bonnie's direction and opens the door. "Bye Mom. Love you. Oh, and check out the spare room sometime. I made some progress last night. Bye Bonnie." She waves and out he goes.

"Hmm," Clara says and walks over to the spare room door. "Wow," she says. Bonnie scurries up behind her.

The desk is clear of all boxes on the left, and a table and chairs have been unearthed and arranged by the window across from the door. Clara almost forgot there was another window in the place. The sun is streaming in and warming up the room. Her grandson's frog painting has been re-hung over the desk. Clara's laptop sits on the desk, with cords attached and connected to outlets underneath.

There's no sign of the boxes he unpacked or the donation pile in front of the spare bathroom. He must have cleared them out. There are a few shiny bobbles carefully placed on the desk and at the table. The spare room, she sees, is more white than beige and her treasures look somewhat passable in this light.

Against the wall across from the desk, to the right, Peter has stacked the remaining boxes neatly, about three high; a manageable height for Clara to tackle. Suddenly, the room is not so overwhelming. She turns to Bonnie and gives her a hug, embarrassed about the tears stinging her eyes.

"He's a keeper," Bonnie says.

Chapter 11

"Do you even know where he lives?" Clara asks Bonnie once they step into the elevator.

"I don't. He's almost always in the lobby, the smoking area, or the diner."

The elevator stops at the second floor and the doors open to a spectacle. Her hair is yellow today. Not blond, but yellow, like marigold yellow. She's wearing a Predators hockey jersey over thick orangey-yellow leggings that could also be tight sweat pants, and yellow Reebok sneakers. "Hi Radish," Clara says.

"Hey guys," Radish says. "Did you get your jump?" she asks Clara. She pushes the first floor button again, and the doors close.

"No, but my son is working on it. Thanks for the name of the garage, by the way."

"No problem," Radish says. "You going out?"

"We're looking for Jimmy," Bonnie says. "We haven't seen him in awhile. Thought he might be in the lobby."

"The guy you were with the other day in the lobby?" Radish says.

"Yes. He always wears a baseball cap," says Bonnie.

"And jeans with holes," say Clara.

"I'll let you know if I see him," Radish says, as the doors open. They walk out together past the mailboxes. The manager's office is open, and Patrick is in there.

"Oh, you're not working today," Clara says.

"I have school," Radish says.

Patrick comes out of the office just then. He has a form with a clipboard. "Radish," he says as she heads for the doors.

She turns around. "Hi Patrick."

"You left the gender question blank on your application here. Want me to fill it in for you?"

She gives him a wry smile. "Nice try. I don't subscribe to gender," she says, and walks out the doors.

Bonnie widens her eyes at Clara. Clara gives her a what are ya gonna do look. Patrick just stands there, furrowed brow, vacant stupid Buzz Lightyear look.

"Patrick, did you take the toys out of the box?" Clara asks. She looks over the lobby. No Jimmy.

"What toys?" says Patrick.

"Never mind. Can we talk to you about something important?" asks Bonnie.

"Fine," he says, and retreats back into his office. He sits behind his desk and gazes at the computer screen while Bonnie and Clara stand there.

"Patrick," Clara starts, "have you heard any rumors about Jimmy?"

Patrick looks at them both. "I don't get caught up in the tenant shenanigans."

"That's good, because rumors are stupid," says Clara.

Patrick continues to stare blankly at his screen.

"People are saying he's a sexual predator."

Patrick drags his eyes away from the computer and settles

them disconcertingly on Clara. "I thought you just said rumors are stupid."

"They are. I think it's causing Jimmy a lot of pain though. Is there some way to fact check it or something?"

"Fact check a rumor?" Patrick says.

"Never mind," Clara says. "I also want to report attempted murder."

Patrick blinks. Eyes Clara warily. Blinks again. "This about squirrels?"

"No, a dog," Bonnie says.

"Ladies," Patrick says, "I know it may be hard to believe but I'm a little busy here. Is this urgent?"

Clara sits down at one of the chairs near his desk. Bonnie sits in the other one. "We can make an appointment," Clara says.

"Fine," Patrick says. "How's...he scrolls through his screen...tomorrow at three o'clock?"

Bonnie starts to nod. Clara says, "No we're busy then." Bonnie melds her positive nod slowly into a negative head shake. "Got anything after five?"

"I leave at five," Patrick says.

"Oh, that's too bad," Clara says.

"Radish is here then," Patrick adds.

"Perfect," says Clara. "We will see Radish tomorrow at five. Wanna jot that down?"

Patrick rolls his eyes. "I'll send her a text."

Out in the lobby, Bonnie and Clara sit by the window, near Jimmy's usual chair. Clara seems pleased with herself and Bonnie is confused. "Mind telling me what that was about?" Bonnie says.

"Oh, he's a dolt. I'm done dealing with him," says Clara.

"Radish will know what to do about Jimmy. And I'd rather file my attempted dog murder complaint with her." Clara looks around the lobby. The silence is disconcerting. "Maybe we should check Jimmy's room. Bonnie, you awake?"

Bonnie's eyes fly open. "What?"

"Tired or something?"

"Not really. I was checking the eyelid scene."

"Can I see your paintings?"

"Promise not to laugh?"

"What could be funny about the back of your eyelids?"

"Ha, ha. OK let's go."

As they pass Patrick's office, Clara stops. "Hey Patrick," she says. He lifts his eyes from his computer screen laboriously. "What's Jimmy's room number again?"

He pauses. Seems to weigh his options.

"Jimmy is one of our best friends," Clara says, sensing a problem. She sits down in front of his desk again. "Did I not tell you how we met? It was one of those cold, November days. Remember Bonnie?"

"Please," Patrick says. "Spare me," and he pulls up a file, clicks on it and scrolls. "Two-oh-nine."

"Patrick, thank you. They broke the mold when they made you," says Clara.

They get off at two and knock on Jimmy's door.

"He doesn't have a wreath," Clara says.

Bonnie looks around. No wreaths anywhere. "Our floor is special, I guess?" They knock again. No answer.

"Well that's that," says Clara, and they head for the elevators again. "Hey, you never told me why you wanted to go to Tai Chi in the first place."

"Aside from how fun it is?" says Bonnie.

"Yes, aside from that."

"I used to go to this Physio guy, Kevin. He's young and handsome and compliments me a lot."

Clara stops, looks Bonnie up and down. "Are you telling me you had eyes for a youngster?"

"No, nothing like that," says Bonnie. "He's engaged actually. Probably married by now. He just made me feel good. He helped me with my shoulder. I wrecked it playing tennis." They push the elevator button. "Anyway, my doctor won't sign off on any more physio for me because he wants me to try Tai Chi first. No Tai Chi, no insurance for physio."

Clara shakes her head. "The things we do to entertain ourselves." She sniffs. The elevator doors open. "Hold on a minute, Bonnie. Do you smell that?"

"What?"

"Smoke."

"Like fire?"

Clara sniffs at the door across from the elevator, looks at Bonnie, and shakes her head. She sniffs at the next door. I must be imagining it, she thinks. Maybe I'm craving a cigarette. She sniffs at the next door. "Bingo," she says. "Who lives here?"

"I don't know. Why?"

"Someone's smoking in there," Clara says.

"So?"

"Peter says I'll get kicked out if I smoke in my place. I thought I was the only one who..." Bestie or not, Clara doesn't want to give Bonnie any fodder for rumors. "...didn't know we couldn't smoke in our apartments. Until Peter told me. About the rule."

Bonnie knocks on the door.

"What are you doing? You crazy or something?" Clara says.

"You didn't know until Peter told you. How is this person supposed to know unless someone tells them?"

Clara drops her jaw in disbelief. "Wow. You really do like everyone."

"I don't like you," Bonnie says. "You're mean."

Just then the door swings open. A giant cloud of lavender air freshener hits them smack in the face. They close their eyes and rub, cough into their elbows, then peer over their arms at the offending tenant. To Clara's horror, it's the creepy guy.

"Oh, hi, Willie," Bonnie says.

Clara grabs her by the arm and drags her toward the stairway. "Sorry to bother you," she says while pulling. "We were looking for someone else. Wrong door, ha ha. Have a good day, sir."

"What was that?" Bonnie says in the stairwell.

"It's him," Clara says. "He's the one who tried to run over Pig."

"So you're scared of him?"

"Kinda," Clara exclaims with sarcasm. "In that he TRIED TO KILL MY DOG."

"Oh." They stare at their feet a minute and listen for movement outside the stairwell door. "We have to take the stairs now, don't we?"

Clara is already trudging up the stairs. Bonnie sighs and follows.

"What are you going to do now?" Bonnie asks when they get to the hallway space between their apartments.

"See your art, of course."

"Oh," Bonnie says, taking out her key.

"And then I'm going to file a complaint against Willie. The sooner he is out of here, the better."

"That sounds about right," Bonnie says and opens the door.

The moment Clara steps inside, she feels she's in another world. No wonder Bonnie is so perky all the time, she thinks. There is no furniture, no TV, nothing (aside from the crappy little kitchenette all the apartments have) but art. Giant, wall-sized masterpieces line the walls left and right. No curtains or blinds on the window, and light pours in, highlighting the vivid colors.

Clara can't even think how to describe it. The patterns are cellular almost, but in a geometric kind of way. She is reminded of wrought iron gates and cursive letters and graceful palm trees swaying in the breeze on a beach. Sun-drenched flowers that morph into bursts of magenta and chartreuse... These indescribable scenes line the walls, leaning up against each other, and several are in progress in the middle of what should be the living room floor. Clara thinks about her dreary apartment carpet upon which she has layered what she thought was a cheerful area rug. Bonnie's living room floor is stripped down to the cement, or wood, or whatever it is, with layers of paint and overlapping patterns dappled on top.

"This is what you see behind your eyes?" Clara says.

"Well, not exactly. I can't take a Polaroid of my eyelids, and it disappears when I open them, so I spend a lot of time chasing after an elusive image. What do you think? Pretty crazy I know."

"I think-"

"Wow, says a voice behind them." Jimmy stands in the door, jaw open, eyes wide.

"Jimmy, we've been looking for you," Clara says.

"I heard. By the looks of Patrick, you've been annoying the bejeezus out of him. I'm back now though. Took me all day, but I found a lawyer to sue the rumor spreaders around this place.

Shit's going to hit the fan, pardon my speech, but we'll be half way to Florida by then."

Bonnie rummages around in the fridge, pulls out a bottle of champagne. "Time to celebrate?"

"Later," Clara says. "I have to make a complaint of my own."

Last thing she remembers is swivelling around to leave, then the swivelling keeps on going until a blur of paint and faces fade to black.

Next thing she remembers is Bonnie and Jimmy standing over her with concerned faces. Snap, snap. Jimmy's hand is two inches from her eyes. "Is she ok?" comes a sing-song voice that can only belong to Bonnie. Snap, snap. Bonnie's hand now. Clara smacks Bonnie's hand, and Bonnie jumps back with alarm.

"Get your hands out of my face," Clara says. "What's wrong with you two?"

"You passed out," Jimmy says.

"She wasn't out, I don't think," Bonnie says.

"What do you call it then?" Jimmy asks Bonnie. "She fell over dizzily into my arms on her way to the floor. Dead weight in my arms, I might add. It's a wonder she didn't pull my back out of joint. And how many times did we ask her 'Are you ok?' with no response?"

"She got dizzy and had a little rest?" says Bonnie.

"All right, all right. I get the picture," Clara says. "What time is it?"

Bonnie looks at her watch. "Two o'clock."

"Right. I skipped my lunch meds again. I got a little dizzy. Have I eaten today?" Clara asks.

"You made Peter some coffee, I think," says Bonnie help-fully. "Other than that, I ..."

Clara is up like a shot. "Pig. He hasn't been walked." She opens the door and wonders why the hallway looks so weird.

"She's doing it again," Bonnie says.

Jimmy and Bonnie each take an elbow and escort her across the hall. When they open the door, Pig comes barrelling across the room, barking crazily, then starts his dancing on the linoleum.

"Hey, Pig, it's okay buddy. We're here now," Jimmy says, and leads Clara to the couch. "You got this?" Jimmy says once she is sitting. "I'm going to take Pig out."

"Got it," Bonnie says.

"What are you two fussing about now?" Clara asks.

Bonnie gets up and grabs the pill box and the almost full can of SlimFast off the counter. The AM meds are gone. She takes out the noon ones and hands them to Clara. She swallows them and takes a few swigs of the drink. "Yum, Bonnie. That's good stuff, thank you."

Bonnie looks at her skeptically. "Can I make you a sandwich or something?"

"I like toast. But first a little nap, I think." She grabs a blanket off the arm of the couch and curls up on her side. Bonnie covers her with the blanket and she's out.

When she wakes up, Bonnie is putting a plate of toast on the coffee table. "Get any dream mail?" Bonnie asks.

Clara shakes her head, sits up and rubs her eyes. Pig rests at the other end of the couch slow-wagging his tail. Jimmy hands her a glass of water.

"I hate water," Clara says.

"You really should drink more water," says Jimmy. "My daughter tells me all the time us old folks get dehydrated easily. And she says vodka-and-water doesn't count."

"That may be," says Clara, "but I hate water." He doesn't take the glass out of her face. They have a small stare off.

Finally, Jimmy says, "Want me to pour vodka in it?"

"Oh give me that," says Clara. She takes a bite of the toast and washes it down with water. Makes a face. "I like butter on my toast," she says to Bonnie.

"Ok, she's back to her old self," Bonnie says to Jimmy.

Clara looks up at the space between the cabinets and the ceiling in the kitchen. Still no goddam clock. "What time is it?" she asks.

"You know your phone has the time on it, right?" Bonnie says.

"You know your wrist has the time on it too, right?" says Clara.

"Little after four," Bonnie says.

"I'm going to go make my complaint now, before I lose my senses entirely," Clara says.

Patrick is typing at his computer when she walks into his office and helps herself to a seat. "No entourage?" he says blandly.

"They're in the lobby," Clara says. "Look, this is serious, Patrick. I need your full attention."

He stops typing, swivels his monitor toward the wall, and leans back in his chair. "Ten minutes," he says.

"Thank you. That is almost human of you, Patrick."

He gives her a don't push it kind of look.

She clears her throat. "Last night, while I was throwing away a poop bag, because that's what I do, is throw away poop bags–"

"As one does when one gets a warning letter regarding apartment rules, I'd hope," Patrick interjects.

Clara sighs. "Anyway. While I was in the dumpster room,

66

which is really dark and not very safe, by the way, especially if it's so creepy your dog won't even go in there–"

Patrick looks at his watch. "Eight minutes."

"Willie Wedge tried to run Pig over with his car," Clara blurts. "I want to file an official complaint."

"What does tried mean?" Patrick says.

"Aimed his car in the direction of my dog. Gunned it. Pedal to the metal. Straight for him," Clara says.

"What's his car look like?"

"What does my car look like?"

"I don't know because I've never seen you aim it at someone or something."

"Look, I know it was him. I saw his face as he left the garage after almost hitting poor Pig. Pig was a shaking bundle of nerves after. Willie filed a complaint about the whole poop bag nonsense – admit it – and he has some kind of vendetta against Pig and me."

"The security cameras–"

"You really pour through hours of video from those cameras to find poop bag offenders?" Clare says. "I thought those cameras were for our safety. Are you going to waste your precious time pouring over more video to confirm the car that almost hit my dog belongs to Willie Wedge?"

"This isn't an apartment rule matter, Clara. This is a criminal accusation. If you are serious about this, you will have to file a police report. Is that what you want?"

Clara thinks for one second. "Yes. He should not be living here. He is dangerous."

"All right then, I'll notify the police. They will want to come interview you. You aren't going anywhere in the next few days, are you?"

"What?"

"If you're a witness to a crime, you have to stick around until the investigation is complete, of course."

Clara swallows. "Of course."

Chapter 12

When she gets to the lobby, Jimmy and Bonnie are sitting by the window with Radish.

"Good afternoon, Radish," Clara says. "How was school? I love you in yellow, by the way. Very cheerful."

"Thanks," says Radish. "I'm into monochrome. How'd it go with Patrick?"

"We were just talking about the parking garage incident," Bonnie explains.

"That's f'd up," says Radish. "Dude trying to take out your dog."

"Right, it was," Clara says, but without enthusiasm. "Thing is, I have to file a police report, which means there will be an investigation."

"Right on," says Radish. "You go, girl."

"Thank you, Radish. I appreciate your encouragement. I really do." Clara looks at Bonnie and Jimmy. "I have to stay in town until the investigation is over."

"Oh," says Bonnie.

"We were planning a road trip," Jimmy says to Radish.

"Florida?" says Radish.

"Good memory," Clara says. "I'm sorry guys."

"We got nothing but time," Jimmy says. Clara smiles, wants to hug Jimmy for being so kind.

"Is that what you wanted to meet with me about?" Radish says. "At five tomorrow?" She holds up her phone with the text from Patrick.

"Um no," Clara says. She locks eyes with Bonnie. "That's a more delicate matter. We can talk about that later."

"Say," Bonnie says, changing the subject, "what did you mean this morning when you told Patrick you don't subscribe to gender?"

"Not that there's anything wrong with that," says Clara.

"Right. Whatever it means," says Bonnie.

Radish laughs. "It's a new concept for your generation, I know. Haaaaaa." She sighs. "Gender is a core sense of self."

"So you're gay?" Jimmy says. "Our generation understands gay. You don't have to tiptoe around it."

"Not really. To be gay, I'd have to identify with a gender. Say, male. And then I'd have to feel that my preferences, sexually, revolve around other men." Radish looks around at their blank faces and tries again. "You can't always tell a person's gender just by looking at them, right?"

"Well, usually," Clara says. "I am pretty sure Jimmy is a man."

"Thank you," says Jimmy.

"Can you tell by looking at him that he has a penis?" Radish says.

Jimmy puts his hands up. "Woah, woah, woah."

"Sorry," says Radish, "too personal. I'll use myself as an example. Can you tell if I have a penis just by looking at me?"

The three of them search each other's faces for the right thing to say here. Jimmy looks at the ground, and Bonnie's cheeks turn a little pink. Clara considers checking under Radish's jersey.

"You're obviously a girl, right?" says Clara.

"The fact that you have to ask to be sure means you can't really tell from the outside," Radish explains. "That's why I don't believe in gender identity because I don't think it matters. I am Radish. The person. Gender just brings with it all sorts of baggage I have no use for."

The three nod in unison. They keep nodding. Jimmy starts to stay something, then just continues nodding.

"Well, you look good in yellow, Radish," Clara says at last. "Wait, is that ok to say?"

Radish laughs. "You guys are a hoot. Listen, ask me whatever you want whenever, but I need to bounce. I have a test in Econ tomorrow. Have a great evening and I'll see YOU two tomorrow," she says to Clara and Bonnie.

Chapter 13

Clara-Clarita-Margarita, How the hell ARE you? It's not what you think up here, trust me. I can't get ANY information about the goings on in your part of the universe, let alone down under (know what I'm sayin'?)!

You aren't seeing that Glen guy anymore, I hope, speaking of down under. He was not going to let up on that request. I kept telling you we are too OLD for that kind of stuff. Hope you found yourself a nice gentleman with a REALISTIC perspective on sex in the senior years. Like we wanna be feeling about in those raggedy ol' loose skin nether-regions only to realize that kind of START gets you a night that NEVER ends. Am I right?

Have to hand it to you, though, you stuck with that online dating business longer than I did. Had yourself some kick-ass dates too! That one man, Charles was it? Took you to the symphony that reminded you of your piano competition days and was so beautiful you had to hide your tears from him...Girl, that was a tender story right there. Then he told you his wife had Alzheimer's and their relationship was down to weekly visits to a person he didn't know any more and vice versa. And I thought you were going to plow right on ahead with that one! You went dancing at the Shriners Club or some nonsense. He took you to fancy restaurants too. What's not to like there? But then you got all sad about the kissing being so meaningful and kept worrying about what his wife would think if she were in her right mind, and then what YOU would think if you were her...

Well. You met some good ones, that's for sure. Sorry I had to spoil all your fun by getting cancer, not that you ever let on, but I know it wore on you. I can't thank you enough for the stories you brought to me about those crazy men. Hoo-boy, we laughed until our sides ached. There I was all hooked up to those vicious chemicals, puking my guts out, and you were right there with me every time, giving me one laugh after another. I tell you what, you were the best friend I ever had. I'm serious. Had lots of friends in my lifetime, not a one of them like you. So. I do hope you found someone special, Margarita.

Life gets so damn hard there toward the end. I had you to soften the blow. And I *pray with all my heart you got some of that sweet friendship love too down there. The rules here are basic. Be at peace. You can't go back. Love yourself. It's like a damn yoga convention. Right, can't cuss either so scratch that last part.*

Did you ever get over your fear of traveling, I wonder? How many times did we talk about saying f-, um chuck-it, let's fly off to Mexico. Let's just DO this. Drink margaritas on the beach. Feel the sand in our toes. Pick up shells in the ocean. Every time we went in those little shops and you wanted to buy some shined up old sea shell I said, let's go get one ourselves, let's go to the SOURCE, girl! You'd laugh and put that bobble down and get all excited. Then we'd get down to brass tacks with the flights and hotel plans and there'd be one excuse after another from you. Arthritis in your fingers. Fungus in your toenails. Showing me articles about plane crashes. It took me awhile to catch on you are NOT the traveling type. And that's okay, my friend, because we had us some fun dreaming up those trips.

You were a good sport, too, when I dragged you to that Chi Chi's for some delicious seafood nachos. You thought I ordered virgin margaritas, but come on, who orders something like that with no tequila? Well, that was a long night propping you up by the

toilet, I tell you...You were right. You
are not a drinker. Both ends too, now that
was impressive.

Well. I'm just writing to say I love you,
Clarita-margarita. That's about the only
thing they let us do around here is love,
and I'll admit, that's ok with me. You live
it up while you're there. Promise? 'Cause
I'll be waiting for some good stories when
you get here. You're one special lady, I
mean that too. Love, Liz

This was the most real letter yet, Clara thinks. She reads it again and lets herself laugh more than cry. The Chi Chi's story is actually funnier the second time. She was so angry at first that Liz tricked her. She has such trouble with her stomach anyway. But thinking about it now, she'd do it all over again just to hear Liz tease her about it the rest of her life.

Clara doesn't want to wake up this time, so she looks up in the pine tree once more for the squirrel. To her delight, it is back, alive this time, chattering at her from one of the branches. On another branch she sees a grey one. The two of them swish their tails at each other in that taunting way squirrels do. Then they are off, chasing each other around and around the trunk, climbing higher and higher until she can hardly see them. One takes a big leap to the next tree, barely catching a spindly branch as it scrambles gracefully to the next one.

Clara wakes up feeling refreshed. But as she looks around and remembers the world she's in, a heaviness settles in around her. She scans the room for Pig and finds him at the door already, ears alert, waiting for a walk. "Just a minute, Pig," she says. She uses the bathroom, dresses, takes her pills and swallows some SlimFast. She eyes the toast by the sink with one bite out of it, throws it away. When she picks up the leash, Pig starts his prancing, and the sound of his happy little linoleum dance connects with the heavy feeling in her heart, taking away a big chunk of it.

Clara stops at Bonnie's door, allowing Pig to trot off, leash dragging behind him, toward the elevator. She closes her eyes and thinks about the vibrant array of colors and patterns on the other side. For fun, she keeps her lids closed a moment longer and tries to focus. But all she sees is darkness, with a sliver of pink she attributes to the hall light above her. When she opens her eyes again, Pig is at her feet looking up at her with confusion and angst. "Ok, ok," she says. "I'm going."

They take the elevator down to the garage as usual and head toward the smoking area. At the last minute, she changes her mind and walks him past the pine tree, down the driveway, to the sidewalk. She pauses there to let Pig sniff around the brush. The snow is gone for now, although the mass of grey sky above threatens to dump a fresh batch. As they stroll down the walk, Pig lifts his leg here and there before choosing a cluster of tired black-eyed-Susans to do his business. She doesn't feel like turning back just yet, so they walk as far as the sidewalk takes them. From there, they cross the street and keep walking. She finds the wooded path behind the community center and keeps going. Pig gives her an excited snort and pulls to pick up the pace. She unsnaps the leash and off he goes, galloping around the trees, darting at phantom critters, lifting his leg at the end of their scented trails.

"You are in your element, aren't you, Pig?" she says. "Sometimes we have to shake it up, I guess."

After awhile, Clara gets a chill from standing around watching her happy little pug and announces it's time to head back. Pig slows down on the way so they take their time, stopping to read the announcements on the community center window, counting the wildflowers that survived the first snow, waving to a handful of other dogs walking their owners. The closer they get to Milton Manor, the more melancholy Clara feels. The lightness she felt reading Liz's letter has gone, and the heaviness weighs on her. She is surprised to find some anger tossing about inside. It's because I hate it here, she thinks. The snow, and the politics, and the gossiping seniors. But that isn't all. She's angry at Liz too. The letter reminded her that she had something to look forward to when Liz was around. There has been nothing to look forward to since.

She remembers hearing the hurt in Peter's voice over the phone after he went on about all the good memories they'd be making when she got to Vermont. She kept telling him she didn't want to move. And he kept telling her how much he loved her and wanted her here. "You're not looking forward to seeing me? To seeing the grandkids?" he said. "No," she said. And she meant it. Before Liz's letter, she couldn't remember the last time she looked forward to anything.

Why make friends when they just leave? Everyone leaves. Being alone means no one can hurt you, Clara thinks. She just wants to be alone, at home, with the ghosts of all who have left her, the ones who cannot hurt her again.

The more she walks and thinks about being forced away from her home against her will, the angrier she gets. When she and Pig make their way up the driveway toward the front doors, they are dragging their feet. She notices the toy scene has changed and stops to take a look.

All the figures face away from each other. They are arranged in a dilapidated circle large enough to accommodate them all, even the frogs. Each facing out, looking at nothing. The snake is the only one on the inside.

Clara and Pig walk through the doors and are greeted by no one. The manager's door is closed. They ride the elevator alone. Pig is too tired to snort his anticipation. The light flickers, as they walk down the hall. Clara lets Pig in and watches him climb the couch with more effort than usual and collapse in an exhausted heap.

She goes to the spare room and takes a box off the top of one of the piles along the wall. She stabs it with the scissors from the desk and rips it open. The first thing she sees is a seashell. She doesn't bother to look at the rest. She turns the box upside down and dumps it out in a clatter of breaking glass and tumbling parts. She picks up the empty box and brings it all the way down to the lobby. The manager's door is still closed, and there is still no one holding court in the lobby. She walks out the doors with the box and loads all the toys into it one-at-a-time. She takes the full box back through the front doors to the elevator and pushes the down button. She gets off in the garage and heads for the door to the dumpsters. She opens the first dumpster she sees and throws the box with the toys into it.

She makes her way back to her room, turns on the TV and finds FOX News, watches the comforting news strip scrolling across the screen. She looks out the window and notices, unlike the others, her car has been cleared of snow. Intrigued, she heads back downstairs to see if it will start.

Chapter 14

She brings her purse, her pillbox and her peacoat just in case. Once inside the car, she takes a deep breath and exhales. "Here goes nothing," she says, and turns the key. It catches, and the motor purrs to life. A tingle of excitement ripples from her head to her toes. "Where to?" she asks her reflection in the rearview mirror.

"When was the last time I drove myself to breakfast?" her reflection says back.

She reverses out of the parking spot, navigates the driveway easily and sets a course for the diner. There are three people in the diner, each eating alone in booths by the window. She is grateful she doesn't recognize any of them, and chooses a table by the wall. She orders two eggs over medium, bacon, and a short stack of pancakes with Aunt Jemima syrup, not real. She eats every bite of the eggs and bacon. The pancakes taste funny, so she sends them back. The waitress brings her toast with butter. The jelly caddy has no seedless blackberry jam, so she eats her toast plain. The waitress brings her a second cup of coffee and the bill. Clara pays for it with some of the one-hundred-dollars Peter gave her and uses the bathroom on the way out.

When she gets in the car again, she doesn't want to go back. So she turns left, instead of right, toward the interstate. She passes a sign for Creamies and another that says Free French Fries Friday and is sorry she ate all her breakfast. She gets to the intersection for the on-ramp and reads one sign for I-89 South, and another for I-89 North. Florida is south, so she chooses the South one. She drives in the right lane. Three cars pass her, so she drives a little faster. She passes signs for Essex Junction, Burlington, and South Burlington. She is starting to feel tired, so she pulls off at the next stop and looks for a place that serves coffee. There are no McDonald's or diners. Only trees, water every now and then, fields with cows and one with chickens.

Finally, she sees a place that is part gas station, part Green Mountain coffee. She parks and orders a coffee with cream and sugar. She sits at a tipsy table near the bathrooms and drinks her coffee. It's too strong but she drinks it anyway. She enjoys the freedom to decide whether to drink strong coffee or not. Whether to drive or not. Whether to spend what little money she has or not. She uses the bathroom, gets into her car and heads back along the road she came towards the Interstate.

It takes longer than she thinks it should and she starts to wonder if she is lost. Eventually, she sees the Interstate on-ramp signs and chooses I-89 South again. She drives for another hour and starts to get tired again. She pulls off after she sees a hotel sign. The room costs $155.35. She counts, and all she has is $91.04. She uses her debit card and the attendant hands her a key for Room 105. Her room faces the woods, not the road, and she is grateful. She lays on top of the beige comforter and falls asleep right away. When she wakes, the sun is low in the sky and she is worried about driving in the dark. She decides she's had enough and chooses the I-89 North sign this time.

The sun sinks lower, and her speed gets slower. Just after the Essex Junction sign, she hears sputtering sounds from the car engine. Shortly after that, she runs out of gas, and manages to guide the car to the shoulder on the highway before its momentum dies off.

It's darker now. A knot of panic forms in her chest. Her car shudders with each passing vehicle and she's afraid to get out. She is grateful when the police car with friendly red lights pulls up behind her and parks. The officer is a woman and asks for her license and registration. These are from Florida, the woman cop says, and hands them back to her. She asks her to take a ride with her in her car, and Clara is grateful for the company.

She sits in a waiting area until another officer asks her if there is someone he can call to come pick her up. She gives him Peter's name and asks if she can file a criminal complaint while she's there. The officer asks what crime, and she says attempted dog murder.

After a while, Peter shows up and looks relieved instead of angry when he sees her. That reminds her to take her pills, but she realizes she left them in the car. Peter and the officer have a long discussion. When Peter comes out, he says, "It's time to go home."

"To Florida?"

He shakes his head and opens his car door for her.

"I forgot my pills in the car," she says, and he shakes out the right amount of noon pills she missed from a bag in the back seat. He opens up another bag and hands her a Slim Fast.

When they get back to Milton Manor, there is no one to greet her. Pig has pooped in the shower, so she cleans it up while Peter walks him.

"I have to go now," Peter says, when he gets back, so she curls up on the couch with Pig and watches the scrolling news tape until she falls asleep.

When she wakes in the morning, the channel is on CNN, and her pill box is back on the counter. She looks, but Peter isn't there. In the spare room, he has cleaned up the mess she made with the box. Pig does his happy linoleum dance, so she finds a poop bag and his leash.

Clara literally bumps into Bonnie outside her apartment door. Bonnie was just about to knock when Clara opened the door, throwing Bonnie off balance and into Clara's arms. Pig barks at both of them madly, circling them, as Bonnie exclaims, "Where the hell have you been?"

"Holy hell Bonnie," you scared me, Clara says, giving Bonnie a little shove after ensuring she is unhurt and set right again.

Bonnie playfully shoves Clara back. "Serves you right for abandoning us all day. Where did you go?"

"Oh Bonnie, it's a long story. Can we please talk about it later?" Clara asks.

"No we can NOT," Bonnie says, standing between Clara and the elevator to block her passage.

Clara sighs. "Fine. Will you at least let poor Pig relieve himself? You can come with us if you like."

"Darn right I'm coming with you," Bonnie says. "Stay right there while I grab my sweater. She opens her door and immediately pokes her head out again. "I mean it, don't you move an inch."

"I am Mt. Everest," Clara says.

"What?" Bonnie says.

"A mountain for Pete's sake, Bonnie, an immovable...Get your damn sweater."

Bonnie is back in a flash. "So start talking," she says, as they walk to the elevators. "You said it's a long story, and I don't have all day."

"Why? What do you have going on?" Clara asks.

"Fine, I have all day," says Bonnie. "But talk fast because I have news of my own."

"What? What happened?"

The elevators open and they step on. "You first."

"It's actually not such a long story," Clara announces, as they arrive at the pine tree and watch Pig snuffle about. She starts with the dream letter from Liz, and by the time they get to the tree, she has finished telling her about the police station.

"Is your car still on the Interstate?" Bonnie asks.

"I have no idea. But I can tell you I am in no mood to go driving today, that's for sure."

"You and Liz were pretty close, huh?"

"Pretty close." Clara shakes her head to avoid going down that path again. "But not as close as you."

"You mean it?" Bonnie says.

"You're right across the hall. How close do you want to be?" Clara says and gives her a little shove. Before Bonnie can tell her how mean she is, Clara adds, "Now. What is your news?"

"Oh. My. God. You won't believe it," Bonnie says. "First off, I talked to Radish, ALONE by the way..." She pauses to give Clara her best hairy-eyeball look.

"Oh get on with it," says Clara. She bends down to scoop Pig's poop and heads toward the dumpster room, tying off the bag as they walk. "Sorry I wasn't there."

"You should be. So first I asked her ... him ..."

"Maybe we should just say Radish rather than her or him?" Clara suggests.

"OK, good idea. I asked Radish if Radish had any suggestions for cheering up poor Jimmy with the whole rumor business. Radish checked some sex offender list on the computer and confirmed that Jimmy's name is nowhere on it. After that, Radish sent around a memo to every tenant in the building scolding them about spreading rumors and making it crystal clear that no tenant living in the building is on any sex offender list and anyone who suggests otherwise better come talk to Radish before spreading baseless rumors and ruining innocent people's reputations." Bonnie takes a breath.

"That is amazing. Good job, Bonnie. What did Jimmy have to say about all this?"

"I was about to say. About the time Radish's memo hit the mailboxes, a bunch of those gossipers were served papers from Jimmy's lawyer suing them for slander."

"Wow, that's big."

"And that's not all."

After Clara throws out the poop bag, the three of them get half way to the elevators when Willie Wedge arrives on the floor, loaded down with boxes. It's too late to avoid him by the time they make eye contact, so Bonnie goes quiet, and they continue toward the elevators as slowly as they possibly can. They are just about to pass Willie's car when he gets there, stops in front of them and sets down the boxes. "Clara. Bonnie," he says.

The two just stand there, speechless. Finally, Bonnie says, "Can I give you a hand there, Willie?"

He opens the trunk and allows her to place one of the lighter boxes inside. As she does so, Willie whispers in Clara's ear, "You'll regret this."

When they get in the elevator, Clara unloads an explosion of nerves explaining to Bonnie what just happened. And that's when Bonnie tells her what Radish did about the attempted dog murder.

"First of all, Radish loves dogs, did you know that? Radish adores them," Bonnie says.

"I'm not surprised," says Clara.

"I told Radish what happened to you and how we were going to have to stick around and wait for the criminal complaint process because dumb old Patrick couldn't do anything else for you. Radish completely disagreed with Patrick on that one and started playing over the video surveillance tapes. Radish matched up one nearly running poor Pig over in the parking garage with Willie's car and made a copy of it. Then Radish delivered it to Willie personally and said, 'Get out.'"

"Radish did all that?" Clara says.

"I kid you not."

"Thank God for Radish."

"Amen. Hey, Jimmy and I were going to have some champagne last night but you weren't anywhere to be found. So we saved it. Because we can finally have a toast and plan our road trip now, right?"

Chapter 15

Later, as Clara sits on the couch with Pig, she thinks about how Peter fixed up her car and she never thanked him for it. Then she thinks about how he picked her up from the police station, was ready with her medicine plus the drink she likes, and cleaned up the spare room mess. She didn't thank him for that either. She can't even remember if she thanked him for that night he transformed the spare room from a bleak warehouse disaster to a tidy, usable space while she slept. The shame she feels eclipses the list of complaints and demands she launches at him every time he comes to visit.

She wonders why he never brings his wife and kids around, and at the same time feels the sting of regret for never having asked about them. Her anger for the place she is in life is all his fault, as far as she is concerned, and his willingness to take her abuse confirms his guilt. He didn't have to make arrangements to move her from Juanita's house. He didn't have to work so hard finding a senior home near him that takes dogs and permits smoking on the grounds with such short notice. He could have left her to her own devices. The fact that he wouldn't or couldn't isn't a cross for Clara to bear.

Her mind drifts to the home she shared with Max. It was magnificent. On the golf course, with a year-round pool, a circle of friends for playing cards and trying out exotic restaurants. It was the life she had dreamed about ever since she was a little girl, playing amongst the corn husks on the farm in Indiana. It was the life she imagined she was owed for all the hours she toiled over the piano keys so her parents could ensure her a "so-phisticated" life. But then Max got sick. And after he died, the bottom fell out of the stock market. She lost Max one year and the house the next.

Was it too much to ask that she enjoy the end of her life? She endured the pain of loss over and over again; when her first marriage collapsed, when Sophie died, her parents, Max, Liz, Ray...she took it all like Job. But the house too? The life she and Max built together? Did she really deserve that?

Yes, she went on a spending spree. Yes, she got careless about bills. Yes, she searched for a man to love who could provide for her the way Max had. But the hits just kept coming. And she is not Job, Clara realizes. She did reach a breaking point where she stopped wishing Peter would call or the grandkids would visit, where she hoped the next fall or broken bone would be her last. But Peter had to come drag her off to the worst place she could imagine moving.

So when Bonnie asked if they can plan their road trip now, Clara said yes. And she thinks she meant it.

◆ ◆ ◆

Clara is dozing on the couch in front of the TV when Bonnie knocks on the door. "Come on," she says, "I found him."

Clara dons her best celebrating outfit, a pale gold silk suit with jewelled buttons. She tells Pig to be good, she'll be back, and heads across the hall.

Jimmy is already seated at the kitchenette bar, champagne glass in hand. Clara walks over and gives him a hug. "Congratulations," she says. "You really did stick it to those gossipy good-for-nothings, didn't you?"

"That I did," says Jimmy. He points to his pants to show her he is wearing jeans without holes in them for the occasion. She laughs and points to the baseball hat on his head. He touches the brim. "Well, let's not get crazy here."

Bonnie sets down two more glasses on the bar and pours the champagne. She is wearing a brightly colored floor length gown that shimmers with fruit and floral patterns, which sounds weird, but looks gorgeous in her apartment full of fanciful eyelid art.

"To making new friends," says Bonnie, and clinks her glass with Jimmy's and Clara's.

"To road trips," says Jimmy, and they clink again.

"To hating this place a little less," says Clara. They clink, laugh and shake their heads at the same time.

"Hey," says Bonnie. "Let's go bring Radish a glass. If it weren't for Radish, we would have a dog killer living here and a bunch of people with nothing better to do than spreading rumors."

"Great idea," says Jimmy, and he finds a glass in Bonnie's cupboard.

Radish is just arriving for work as they get downstairs. She is dressed head to toe in pink, including her hair.

"How do you change your hair every day?" Bonnie asks.

"It's just spray color," says Radish. "It washes out."

"Isn't pink a girl color?" says Jimmy.

"Color has no gender," says Radish. She accepts her glass of champagne gratefully, and offers a toast of her own: "To losing our labels," she says.

They clink and Bonnie says, "Oh, I get it, because gender is a label?"

"Lots of things are labels," says Radish. "Anything that makes you feel stuck is a label."

"To hell with labels," says Clara. They clink one last time and drain their glasses.

"Oh hey, did you see the toy scene today? The snake is gone," Radish says.

"What do you mean? I threw away the toys," Clara says. They give her a dodgy look. "They were mine to begin with. I set them out for trash, and someone got to them before the garbage guy, I guess, and used them to make all those crazy scenes."

"Huh," says Jimmy.

"Well, they've been rescued from the garbage again then," Radish says. "Except for the snake."

They walk outside and look at the patio together. The toy figures are back in their dilapidated circle, but instead of facing out, they are facing in. And the snake is missing.

"That's nice," says Bonnie. "Without the snake, they can live together in peace."

"Hey, my car's back too," says Clara. She walks across the lot and opens the door. There's a note on the dashboard from Peter. Gas tank is full, it says, and please apply for your Vermont license and registration.

"He gave you the websites too," Jimmy points out.

"Now we'll have to decide which car to road-trip in," says Bonnie.

"The one with valid license plates?" Jimmy says.

"Because three people, a dog, and luggage is going to be so comfortable in a Kia," says Clara.

"Okay, guys. I better get to work," says Radish. "Someone has to manage the snakes in this place."

Clara feels a little lightheaded and is relieved to see when she gets back she did remember her noon pills. I hope champagne works out better for me than tequila, she thinks, as she snaps on Pig's leash and tucks a poop bag into the pocket of her peacoat.

She heads for the pine tree and considers finding a box for the toys so she can locate a more permanent trash bin for them. Pig takes longer than usual to sniff. Clara gets a chill waiting for him and pulls the collar of her peacoat higher up her neck. Pig concentrates his snuffling an inordinate amount of time at the base of the tree.

"What is the deal, Pig?" she says. "Get on with it."

He looks up at her and snorts. Finally, he poops just as the moon comes out from behind a cloud. She looks up to admire it, thinking that seeing the moon is a fitting end to this lovely day, but she is distracted by something in the tree. About ten feet up where the dead squirrel used to be hangs a doll. Its hands and feet are nailed to the tree to keep it in place. The moon rolls behind a cloud. And when it comes out again, she sees that the doll is Woody from the movie Toy Story.

Chapter 16

No one knows who put Woody in the tree. Radish has the tree cut down and Woody taken with it, as it was slated by the city for removal anyway. Clara unpacks a box of clothes in the spare room and uses the box to pack up the other toys. This time she drives it to the dumpster by the McDonald's, and while she's there, buys a cheeseburger from Radish.

Days go by, and Peter doesn't call or visit. The road trip has been scheduled, and Clara is anxious to connect with Peter to make sure she has enough money for the trip and her medication has been picked up and organized. She calls him and leaves a message, finding it strange he doesn't pick up. He always picks up.

Two days before the road trip, the tires of her car get slashed. The garage says it will cost $200 to fix. Radish suggests she file a complaint with the police this time, but Clara doesn't want to jeopardize her road trip plans. She leaves another message for Peter, telling him about the car and asking about her finances and meds. The day before their trip, he shows up at her door with a binder full of papers and another giant pill box.

They sit in her apartment and drink coffee while Clara fills Peter in on all the events he has missed. He smiles at all the right things and frowns at all the unfortunate things, but something seems off to Clara.

"Are you okay, Peter?" she finally asks. "You aren't still mad about me taking off with the car that one day, are you?"

"Mad?" Peter says. "No, I'm not mad. I do have something to tell you, though."

"Okay," Clara says, and sets her coffee down on the table.

"I brought your finances. Everything you need is right there in that binder. There's a tab for medications too. You'll find your doctors' numbers in there and a list of prescriptions and how many of what to take and when. Kinney's Drugs has all this stuff, too, and they will help you with refills and keeping your pill box organized."

Clara's stomach feels funny and she has an urge to fold something or smoke. Pig is snoring next to her on the couch and she reaches over and scratches his neck.

"I'm moving to Indiana," Peter finally says. "Ryan's wife... Ryan is the one who painted that frog in there..." He points to the spare room. "...his wife is sick, doesn't have long to live actually. He's beside himself, as you can imagine. He could really use some help. And once Katie's gone... that's his wife... he'll need help with his kids."

"Can't you send your wife?" Clara asks.

"Maggie left me several years ago, Mom. She's living in Scotland, remarried. Happy."

Clara tries to smile at that but can't seem to move her face.

"I lost my roofing business. One of my employees hit a little girl, 5 years old, with the company van when he was driving too fast in a residential area. I had to file bankruptcy after the lawsuit. Finding work in Vermont isn't easy. I've been doing consulting work here and there when I can. But I have a good offer with a large construction company in Indiana, so..."

"I'm sorry I never asked about your family, Peter," Clara says. "I'm sorry I–"

"It's fine, Mom. You've had a rough couple of years. I should have said something, but I didn't want to add my troubles to yours."

"How is..." Clara is appalled she can't remember his name. "Ryan's little brother."

"Jack is fine. He's a missionary in India right now. He met his wife in seminary school. They have five kids. They're very happy. Actually, he's the one who gave me the idea about the Woody doll," Peter says. "We FaceTime once a week. He remembered you taking him and Ryan to the movies and how you tried to steer them to the Woody dolls at Target, but they were both crazy for Buzz Lightyear. Funny the things we remember as we get older..."

"What Woody doll?" Clara says.

"You didn't get it?" Peter says.

"I don't think so," says Clara, willing herself not to think about what she saw on the tree after having one of the best days she can remember having.

"That's weird. The night I picked you up from the police station, I stopped by here first for the pillbox and a SlimFast. I put Woody on the counter right there." He points to the bar where she keeps the pillbox. "There was a card, too, with some drawings Jack's kids made for you."

Clara scratches Pig's neck some more but she can't make the ache in her gut go away. "I'm tired now, Peter. I think I'll go to bed now."

"Oh." Peter seems surprised, then hurt, then sympathetic. "Okay. Well if you have any questions, just call me, okay Mom?"

"Okay."

"You're in good hands here, I think."

"Yes, I suppose so."

He gives her a kiss on the top of her head. "I love you, Mom." And he's gone.

Clara turns on the TV and watches the news scrolling by. She shakes a cigarette out of the pack from the decorative vase on the coffee table and lights it with the lighter under her cushion. She wonders what time it is and looks above the cabinets in the kitchen out of habit. There's a clock there now. Peter must have done that too. She doesn't want to know what time it is. She thinks about the place she once was and the place she intends to be again. Then she has herself a good, calming smoke.

THE END

Acknowledgments

For critiquing and improving my work, I am indebted to dear friend and talented writer, Julianna Thibodeaux; as well as Alexandra Kirschbaum, Adrian Larose, Mer Brebner and Nicole Powell of the Ottawa Writers Circle, who said yes when I asked for help; and the Sunnyside Library Writing Workshop members, particularly author in residence Michael F. Stewart. Thanks also to Rob Bignell for ridding my manuscript of the most basic grammatical and literary errors.

For shaping my cover design aspirations, I am grateful for Harry Loop and Suzanne Naudin. For improving my cover design aspirations, I want to thank David Drummond.

I also want to thank my Book Club, without whom my mind would be less enlightened; my husband, Alan, who keeps me grounded and puts out fires while I write; and my parents who encouraged me to keep writing.

About the Author

Mary Ann Tippett is a writer living in Ottawa. She has a Doctor of Jurisprudence degree from Indiana University. "Clara & Pig" is her first published novel.

Made in the
USA
Middletown, DE